THE PROTEU$ AGENDA

BETTY ALT
DAVID CONWAY

Cold Tree Press
Nashville, Tennessee

Published by Cold Tree Press
Nashville, Tennessee
www.coldtreepress.com

© 2007 Betty Alt & David Conway All rights reserved.
Cover Design © 2007 Cold Tree Press

For Lara and Bill

THE PROTEUS AGENDA

Proteus. *Greek Mythology.* A sea god who could change his shape or identity at will. If pursued or captured, he could change to a lion, a boar, a serpent, water or fire...

THE LOS ANGELES PREPARATION

(JULY 1981)

Cold, bitterly cold. A faint dusting of snow cascading through the darkness from trees lining the road. A flash of light from an approaching car as it crests the top of the hill. The blast of a locomotive whistle. The car speeds by. Another bellow from the whistle. Grinding metal, a ball of fire, brakes screeching amid a shower of sparks. Wreckage dragged along the rails and scattered across the frozen ground...

"Excuse me sir, excuse me!" The attractive blonde stewardess persisted, shaking him slightly. "Please wake up, sir, and put your seat back in the upright position for landing."

"Welcome to LAX," the words over the intercom brought him fully awake from his dream. He shook his head and shivered slightly. It had been several years since he had been bothered with the dream. Why now?

As the plane touched down on the runway, a crooning voice interrupted his thoughts. "The current temperature is a balmy 80 degrees. Local time is 7:10 P. M. You can claim your luggage at carousel C. The Captain and crew wish to thank you for flying with American Airlines, and we hope you will fly with us again."

"Sorry" the swarthy man muttered politely to the middle-aged woman whose shoulder he bumped as he attempted to retrieve his well-traveled garment bag and wrinkled raincoat from an overhead bin. "Flying first class should be the only way to go," he mused, instead of being shunted into a tourist section—what he always referred to as the "cattle car" with its cramped space and the unavoidablesounds and smells of humanity crammed shoulder to shoulder. Well, never again. After today it would be first class all the way.

He knew he would be hunted, but no one would find him. Most observers, had any bothered to notice, would have seen the usual veteran of air travel. His clothing, tinted glasses and manner were fully consistent with that of any salesman returning home on a Friday night. While he was slightly taller than most of the other business travelers who had boarded American Airlines flight 409 for Los Angeles, he appeared just as resigned and bored as the rest. Like several other men, he had produced a newspaper, which he pulled apart over his ample lap and had become merely a standard fixture in the plastic world of modern air travel.

However, this man is different from his companions. His appearance and almost everything about him is false. His black hair and swarthy complexion is a result of a wig and deftly applied makeup. His pudgy appearance consists of layers of towels tied securely around his waist, and his eyes are blue behind the dark sunglasses. Unlike most of his fellow passengers in coach, he is very rich. Also setting him apart from the other passengers is his lack of feeling for the things and the people which act as a tether to the rest of society. With indifference he moves through a complicated world of his own making—a changeling with the skills of a modern Proteus.

No one would ever think of looking for him in L.A., he was certain. He had greatly altered his former appearance, had a completely new identity in place and had a safe location in which to stay until he could put the next phase of his plans into operation.

Slowly he edged toward the plane's exit, his tweed garment bag buffering him from the stampede of passengers crowding the aisle. The plane had been filled to capacity, as it usually was on a Friday evening, and he had delayed a little too long getting up from his seat. As he neared the exit door and maneuvered the bag to one shoulder, a young woman brushed against his protruding paunch and briefly met his eyes with an embarrassed smile of apology. Soon, he thought, I'll be rid of this extra bulk around my waist.

"Goodbye. Thank you for flying American," the stewardess beamed her automatic smile as he headed into the waiting area and merged with the crowd.

Finally outside in the pale sunlight filtering through the Los Angeles smog, he joined the throng lined up for taxis. "The Ocean Breeze Motel on Pacific Coast Highway," he told the cab driver and settled back into the seat with a deep sigh. A sour odor from too many passengers mingled with the pine smell emanating from a small cardboard tree which dangled below the rearview mirror. Still, it felt good to get out of the airport crush and to relax for a few minutes.

As the cab left Sepulveda and passed the Wyndham Hotel, he noted a frail, graying woman standing on the corner. His quick glance took in the years of hardship etched in the lines about her mouth and the bent shoulders, as if the burden she carried were too great. For just an instance he thought of his mother and wondered what filled her days now that his father was dead and no longer part of her life. He could picture her years earlier, shoveling drifts of snow from the front sidewalk while his father lay in a drunken stupor. For a moment he felt remorse that he had not done more to make her life easier. Quickly he shook away the thought of her and the shabby neighborhood in which his family had lived. He had no time for memories; they could become a cancer of the mind. A person with a new identity could not afford to have memories.

Cruising along Lincoln, the cab slowed for a car wheeling into the Airport Marina Hotel and then turned onto Highway 10. Traffic became heavier, and he noticed that the white and pink blossoms of the oleander bushes bordering the road were coated with a fine layer of dust from the cars as they churned endlessly up and down the coast.

"Just here for a vacation on the beach?" the cabby asked a few minutes later as the auto pulled into the aging Ocean Breeze motel, its beige stucco walls cracked and weathered by the years of salt spray.

"Yes, I'm just out from New Mexico; never seen the ocean before." He'd never been to New Mexico, but the cab driver obviously expected some kind of response, and, in the extremely remote possibility that anyone ever tried to check on him through the cab company, they would be unable to find any trace. "This is about all I can afford." He paid the driver, adding the small tip that could be expected from a tourist on a strict budget.

As the cabby drove away from the Ocean Breeze, the man turned from the seedy motel, swiftly crossed to the beach side of the highway and walked briskly several blocks south. Even in the gloom of approaching twilight, he could see the waves pummeling the shore but noticed that the roar of the surf seemed muted by the constant clamor of the traffic. The salty breeze was refreshing after the stagnant humidity of Houston; however, the pace of his walk caused him to perspire, and he could feel the tawny make-up on his face beginning to erode. "Just in time," he thought, as he stopped before a large house.

Cautiously surveying his surroundings to see if anyone else were walking near by, he unlocked the door on the multi-level home and entered the spacious foyer. "Just as elegant as I remembered it," he muttered with satisfaction as he moved through the rooms furnished in sturdy rattan and tastefully patterned cushions. A crystal decanter and glasses sat on a small bar nestled in one corner of the spacious den. From the large windows that surrounded three sides of the house he could still make out the surf rolling in only forty yards beyond the deck. To his right he noticed in the gathering dusk the faint silhouette of a woman strolling along the beach, two small dogs ahead of her darting in and out of the surf. Going into the master bedroom he took off the sunglasses that had shielded his blue eyes and peeled the black wig from his head. His hair was matted down, his scalp itchy and damp with perspiration. Carefully he hung the wig on a spigot in the bathtub so that its mesh foundation would have a chance to dry. He would need the wig at a later time.

After stripping to his shorts and removing padding from around his waist, which had given him the obese appearance, he mixed at the bathroom basin a bottle of Clairol #04 and worked it carefully into his normally medium brown hair. While he waited the required 25 minutes for the hair dye to take effect, he extracted from his wallet the driver's license and credit cards of a Mark Proteus, the name he had flown under, and replaced them with a new license and credit cards. Proteus! "Clever name," he said aloud, grinning.

All of the trappings of Proteus were then placed in the garment bag and hung in the closet. Two shirts, a pair of tan slacks, a pair of white shorts, some sandals and a cotton bathrobe made up the rest of his meager wardrobe that had been previously hung in the closet several weeks earlier. His plans included purchasing clothing suitable for his sojourn on the beach, but, if he had to, he could get by for a few days with what was available. He congratulated himself on the setup.

Standing in the shower he scrubbed the dye from his hair and dark make-up from his face, neck and hands and watched the colored water swirl down the drain, destroying any trace of his recent identity. Afterwards he donned the bathrobe, wiped the steam from the bathroom mirror and surveyed his new image—streaked blonde hair, pale skin and blue eyes. "Goodbye Mark Proteus. Hello, Todd Walker," he announced, smiling at his new reflection.

Opening the doors of the oak cabinets in the kitchen, he contemplated the supplies which he had dropped off a month ago—necessary staples and a good number of canned goods. The refrigerator held a six-pack of beer, a few frozen dinners and a bottle of wine. "Well, a frozen dinner and bottle of Riesling will do for tonight," he thought. "Tomorrow I will have to do major shopping, and I need to do some banking."

Following a light supper of Riesling and some taste-less roast beef and rubber vegetables, he stretched out on the ample sofa to enjoy a second glass of wine. Briefly he thought of the past few hours, forcing his mind to critically evaluate and ferret out any mistakes he might have made. There were none. In Houston, he had checked his luggage and received his boarding pass as salesman Bill Robinson, a dutiful husband returning from a week of sales meetings. Then he had simply purchased another ticket and boarded the plane as Proteus. Robinson no longer existed.

From one of the windows he could see in the distance the blue neon sign of his recent employer and last victim, A. A. Cybertech. Raising his glass of wine in a salute, he murmured, "Try and find me!"

Saturday morning dawned warm and clear with a slight breeze off the ocean, just perfect for a quick jog on the beach. Waves collided with the shore, and surfers were already waxing their boards, waiting for the right set. Gulls dipped towards the water, white splashes in the blue sky. Moving slowly to cool off from his run, the recently created Todd Walker climbed onto his deck and sat down to empty sand from his shoes. As he wiped sweat from his face, he glanced around at the other beach houses. He could see tubs of red geraniums dotting decks further down the beach and the scarlet and coral blossoms of bougainvillea climbing over rooftops and up carport walls. Laughter rippled through the air as three small boys scampered from behind a deck and headed for the surf. In the distance he could see a couple strolling by the water's edge, the woman circling around the man as the waves curled toward her feet. He had been right to select this locale, Todd thought. It was a pleasant place to hide while his trail cooled. Suddenly his peaceful reverie was interrupted by a cheery voice calling out to him.

"Good morning." She leaned over her deck railing and pushed large sunglasses up into her hair, her ample cleavage nearly spilling out of a short terrycloth robe. "Just moved in?"

Startled, he looked up. Lost in reverie, he had not heard her approach nor had he prepared himself to meet anyone that soon or that early in the morning. "Late last evening," he said curtly.

"What happened to the other guy I saw once or twice?"

"I don't know. I just moved in last night," Todd repeated.

"Well, welcome anyway." She brushed tendrils of tousled blonde hair back over her shoulder and sipped at a cup of steaming coffee. The coffee mug had some cliché about blondes on it, and Todd wondered how true it could be. He estimated her age to be about thirty-four. "Trying to appear much more youthful than she is," he thought. She didn't quite bat her eyelashes at him, but he felt she might at any minute. Despite his irritation at this unexpected interruption, he was uncomfortably aware of the woman's steamy sexiness. I can't afford this, he thought.

"My name's Tina. Tina Zabinski."

"Todd," he replied tersely, giving his new name and moving toward his door.

"Well, Todd, we must get together later on."

"Sure, we'll do that," he replied with a quick nod as he disappeared through the door.

"Shit," he said aloud as he removed his sweaty jogging apparel. "Just what I need, an overly friendly female neighbor."

Once showered and dressed, he called a cab and headed back to LAX. Waiting for him was the red Ford Mustang convertible that Bill Robinson had reserved earlier in Todd Walker's name. As he filled out the required paperwork for the rental agent, he somehow became aware that he was being watched. Leaning on the counter, he casually turned and looked over his shoulder. A few feet away stood two policemen, and they were both looking directly at him. "I've been found," was his first thought as his breath caught in his throat. Quickly he tossed the thought aside. After all, if they were looking for him, it would be as Bill Robinson, who no longer existed. Besides it was too soon for the police to be involved. He had only been gone a little over twelve hours. Suddenly both policemen laughed as if they had shared a good joke and walked away. Sighing, he relaxed and turned back to the rental counter.

Equipped with transportation, he started on the numerous errands that would help set him up for his stay in Santa Monica. Six months of generally keeping out of sight was what he had planned, and then he could move smoothly on to the next phase of his agenda.

She was waiting for him as he drove up.

He forced a smile. "Hi, Tina. She had changed to white slacks, high-heeled sandals and a skimpy red tube top that did not flatter her waist. A tasteful application of makeup covered the beginning of lines around her eyes that he had noted earlier in the day; her hair was now neatly brushed back from her face and held in place with a red headband. It was, he thought, quite an improvement over the way she had looked earlier that morning. Still, overall, her appearance was just slightly sleazy.

"Oh, I was getting ready to leave soon. I'm so glad you came back now." She bounced over to the car. "Nice car," she purred, running her hand over the back fender. "Did you just get it?"

"You needed something?" Todd asked as he opened the trunk to start unloading sacks of groceries. He was irked that she was in his way again, prying into his business.

"No. I was just going to invite you over tonight. I'm

having a few friends in—just casual, only a small group. Here, let me help you with those things." Before he could respond, Tina took a sack of groceries out of the car trunk.

Todd was caught. He didn't want help, but he didn't feel that he could be rude or do anything that might set him apart from the average Joe citizen who would want to take advantage of what Tina was offering—apparently much more than just help with the grocery bags. After all, Tina was fairly attractive, although a little chubby for his taste, and she was obviously on the make.

He unlocked the door, and she followed him into the kitchen. "I'll put these in the cabinets for you while you bring in the other things."

When he returned, he found that she had settled herself at the bar. "I could go get us a beer, if you don't have any cold yet?"

"That's O.K., Tina. There should be a couple of Heinekens in the fridge. I'll just take these other things up to the bedroom." He left and climbed the stairs, cursing silently. Evidently Tina could become a problem. On the other hand, maybe he was over reacting. Probably she merely saw him as an eligible man, possibly with some money; would it appear odd if he were too abrupt in discouraging her?

Going back into the kitchen, Todd smiled and said, "I'd like to come to your party. What time?"

"Oh, great! Eight-thirtyish, if that's all right. Here's your beer."

"Let's drink it on the deck," he suggested. "I need to work on my tan."

"I noticed you were sort of pale," Tina commented. "Are you just here for a few weeks of vacation?" She sounded anxious.

"No, longer than that. A few months are more like it."

"A few months! I don't even get a month's vacation," Tina said petuantly. "What do you do that allows you to take off from work so long?"

"I'm at work now. I'm a writer. I came out here to finish a novel. I couldn't seem to get it together back in Boston. I thought of Miami, but I decided on sunny Southern California."

"A writer! I think that's so fascinating," Tina gushed. "What's your book about?"

"It's the story of a homicidal maniac, who does in pretty little blondes on the beach—those who pester their neighbors," he blurted. "Dumb," he thought. "Stop babbling and don't be offensive or you could regret it later."

But Tina didn't appear to find his comment offensive. "Oh, you're kidding," she said with a little giggle. She was flattered about the pretty little blonde part. "But I can take a hint. You're telling me that you need to be busy. I won't bother you too much, but remember, all work and no play..." She let the sentence dangle as she finished her beer and got up to leave. "I'll see you around eight-thirty. Don't forget."

Todd watched as, managing to make the trip an erotic experience, she climbed onto her deck. Settling back to finish his beer, he groaned, "Of all the beach cottages on all of the beaches in the world, why did she have to live next to mine?" He had not seen her nor anyone else when he had rented the place and moved in the meager groceries and clothing two months previously. Poor research on my part, he thought to himself. Have to do better in the future. He had been careful to do all of the moving in the late evening and at night. Still, she must have seen him as Bill Robinson at some time or she would not have questioned him earlier about "that other guy". He thought his cover story about needing time to write might discourage her from being too much of a pest, especially if he provided her with some little bit of attention from time to time. As in the past, he could foresee her becoming a problem. "Loose ends; God how I hate loose ends," he grumbled, abstractedly stroking his chin. "I may just have to get rid of this particular loose end."

As the sky began to fade from orange into the lavender of dusk, Todd rose and went into the den. Putting the doubts about the evening party from his mind, he settled at the spacious rattan desk and began to check items off a list. First he had picked up the rental car and had closed his Southern Pacific account under the name of Anthony Stevens, had asked for a Cashier's Check for the $13,700 to be made out to Mark Proteus and then had deposited that money into a Todd Walker checking account at the Wells Fargo Bank on Mindaro Avenue and Lincoln.

Then he had checked on accounts in Miami, Nassau, Grand Cayman, Switzerland and London. The beach house did not have a working phone nor did Todd plan to have it made usable. In case anyone should ask, he could always say that he didn't want any interruptions while writing. Pay phones were safer—no records. However, it had taken him considerably longer to get all of his overseas calls to the various banks completed. Still the extra time was good insurance.

Good! He had accomplished all of the things on his list. Stretching, he wandered back into the kitchen for another beer and returned to the deck. It would soon be time to dress for Tina's party, but he still had at least an hour to relax. Idly, he wondered what his wife Margaret would be doing. He doubted that she would be going to her uncle's scheduled retirement party from Cybertech, especially without her absent husband. He hadn't thought about Margaret since he left on his Cybertech business trip, but, then, he hadn't thought too much about her when he was going home every night. Wouldn't she be incredulous to learn what had really happened to Bill Robinson and that he was only a few miles away. Of course, she wouldn't believe it. Nice woman overall, but so gullible. Poor bitch didn't stand a chance with him. She would be frantic, he knew.

He had not deliberately set out to hurt her. When he originally made his plans years before while still in the Air Force, they had not included a wife nor commitment to any female. His testosterone was within normal limits and he liked women, but you couldn't trust them; they were usually jealous, controlling and blabby. Unlike many of the other airmen, he had avoided street prostitutes for fear of disease. Casual liaisons with women he picked up in bars or night clubs occasionally fulfilled some of his sexual needs; otherwise he did without.

He certainly had no intention of marrying. However, he altered his plans when he settled in at Cybertech and found he could easily siphon some of its funds into his bank accounts without detection. People kept asking why he was unmarried. This made him different from most of the other men with whom he worked, and he didn't want to attract attention, to stand out from the crowd. He had learned several years earlier that blending in with the crowd was the safest defense. Fewer questions were asked. Finally he decided that he needed a more a cceptable facade than that of a single, eligible male. Margaret helped create this.

He had been introduced to Margaret at a church picnic by his boss, Jim Dawson. Margaret was Dawson's niece—unmarried and in her mid twenties.

"You two need to get to know each other," Dawson had stated. "Never know what might come of it."

They had made polite chit chat across a red and white checkered paper tablecloth which a slight breeze kept threatening to strip away. Platters of fried chicken mingled with huge bowls of pimento speckled potato salad, and the two were encouraged by a buxom white-haired woman to take another helping. "You two aren't eating enough to keep a body alive," she chirped, ladling a mound of cabbage slaw and baked beans onto each of their striped paper plates.

As the afternoon wore on, he decided it might be politically wise to show some interest in Margaret. Walking with her after retrieving a slice of Dutch apple pie from the dessert table, he casually said, "If you're not busy this coming Wednesday evening, perhaps we could have dinner and take in a concert."

She had readily accepted, and after four months of dinners, movies and social outings with other Cybertech employees, he had asked her to marry him.

"I'm very happy for the two of you," Dawson had

beamed his congratulations and then insisted on providing his niece with a lavish church wedding complete with a traditional long white gown, a catered dinner for over two hundred guests, and a dance band.

He had not loved Margaret. Actually he could not remember really loving anyone, not his father nor his mother, although he had felt some affection for the woman who had nurtured him. Love! He could not understand the concept.

Still he found little to complain about with Margaret during their months together. She was presentable, personable, and, best of all, naive. She performed adequately in bed, accepted his numerous company-sponsored trips away from home and seldom asked questions about his past. To all appearances he was part of a typical young couple—struggling with finances, trying to get ahead in his job, buying a home. The cover was perfect. He was just an average guy. Too bad that cover had to go. He had gotten accustomed to being Bill Robinson, the Cybertech salesman and computer expert, and the wealth that identity had brought him. "Oh, well," he muttered quietly as he got up to dress for Tina's party. "One can always become someone else."

"Todd, darling." Tina, in a tight, short sundress splashed with gaudy geometric designs, rushed over and kissed him on the cheek. She put her arm possessively around his shoulder, the bright red nails on her hand contrasting sharply with his charcoal gray slacks and pale, blue-striped polo shirt. "How nice of you to come. Let me introduce you to the gang. Everyone! Attention everyone! This is Todd. He's my new neighbor. Isn't that delicious?"

The names and faces were a blur—Larry in a light green leisure suit with a prominent gold chain around his neck; Eloise, a wisp of a woman garbed entirely in white, her hennaed hair teased high with short bangs framing large blue eyes; Jack, older than the rest by a good ten years, in Bermuda shorts and a Hawaiian shirt, possibly an old surfer; Rhonda, Tina's roommate, an attractive woman with black hair hanging well below her shoulder blades and nearly covering up large turquoise earrings. She was dressed much more conservatively than Tina in a black skirt and peasant blouse.

"Rhonda's a commercial artist at an advertising agency and *very talented,*" Tina had explained to Todd when making introductions. Todd noted that Tina had a habit of emphasizing her adjectives and adverbs by raising her voice slightly.

There must have been at least thirty people in Tina's "small group of friends". Todd noted that her and Rhonda's place was slightly larger than his. Adjoining the living area was a solarium on the north side away from his cottage. Bracketed by a high wooden fence, it provided great amounts of light while still insuring privacy. Guests were overflowing onto the deck, grazing the hors d'oeuvres and guzzling mixed drinks.

"So, you're a writer?" Larry asked as he removed a swizzle stick from his drink. Obviously, Tina had not lost any time filling her friends in about Todd.

"Sort of. I'm trying to get a manuscript started."

"Got an agent?" Larry continued. He leaned closer to Todd and said in a boasting manner, "I know a couple of good ones out here. Let me know if you need a word put in for you. I've made some good connections."

"Think I've got one nailed down in Boston," Todd said, trying to move a little further away from Larry and his heavy odor of English Leather aftershave.

"Boston!" Tina exclaimed. "I have an uncle living in Boston. Perhaps you know him. John O'Brien. He lives in Billerica."

"No, I don't think so," Todd replied politely. "After all, it's a rather large city." Jesus! Was this woman for real?

"Do you plan to be here long?" Rhonda asked as she joined the group beginning to surround Tina and Todd.

Her voice was soft and low, a definite contrast to Tina's.

"A few months or so. It depends on how much I get done on the book."

"You don't really have a Boston accent." Jack stated flatly as he extracted an olive from his martini and plopped it into his mouth. His eyes were too close together, Todd noted, making his face appear long and narrow like pictures Todd remembered from childhood books about Ichabod Crane.

"I'm originally from Colorado, a little coal mining town in the southeast," Todd lied, hoping they wouldn't want a detailed blueprint of the town, the mine and the amount of production. "Excuse me a second; I need to get some more ice in my drink."

Todd retreated to the bar to escape the grilling. Tina certainly had some inquisitive friends, much too inquisitive for his comfort. He had already fabricated the author story and wanted to reinforce that as his sole reason for being in California.

"They really are *quite* snoopy, aren't they?" Tina followed him and slid her hand into his. Her fingers were cool and twined around his in shared intimacy. It also, he felt, told the others that she had found him first and to keep hands off.

"They don't mean any harm," she explained. "But you know how it is. Everyone in California is from somewhere else. We all just seem to want to find someone we've known before."

Rhonda had put on a Neil Diamond record, and the men moved some pieces of furniture. Several people began to dance.

"Let's," Todd said, ushering Tina toward the cleared space. Dancing with her at least would keep him out of conversation with the other guests for a while.

Tina was a good dancer and when Diamond was changed for a slow tune, she snuggled cozily in his arms. "Isn't this nice?" she purred. "We could do this often, if you like."

Todd mumbled something appropriate as the music ended and mentioned that they both could use another drink. He and Tina danced again; then he asked Rhonda for a dance and was pleasantly surprised that she seemed comfortable just to move to the music without constantly chattering or questioning him. From the bit of conversation that they did share, Todd decided he might like to know Rhonda better. He could see that becoming a problem, however, as he was aware of Tina's eyes following them around the room. He felt certain Tina would bombard Rhonda with questions about their conversation later that night.

Shortly after eleven, and with loud protestations from Tina and her friends, he explained that he had to be up early as he needed to get things set up to begin writing and took his leave of the crowd. Tina followed him out to the edge of her deck, said she would "see him tomorrow," gave him a lingering kiss, and then hurried back to the party.

He was now certain that Tina was going to be a major complication in his plans as he was sure she would show up the next day as promised. In the midst of all of the questions about him, he had barely managed to learn something about her life. She took voice lessons three afternoons a week and usually worked until midnight as a hostess at a local club. He had noticed that two cars were parked in the women's carport—an old Datsun and a Capri. This led Todd to question the opulence of the two women's beach house. How could Tina's hostess job and Rhonda's advertising position support that place? He knew that rental costs on it would be similar to his house and, since it was larger, probably more. Did Larry and Jack contribute? Did that mean that one or both of the men would be around the beach house quite a bit? Or maybe Tina or Rhonda was divorced and each had gotten a good settlement. Todd would have to ask Tina. Given her penchant for chatting, he was certain she would be only too happy to volunteer this information, and he needed to know who might be coming and going at his neighbors'. He sighed. He had only been Todd Walker for a little over twenty-four hours, and already he was encountering some complications for his plans.

"Mrs. Robinson?" The man spoke softly, his ruddy face with slightly pitted cheeks creased by a slight grin. "I'm Detective Matthews." He showed her his I.D. and badge. "May I come in?"

"Oh, my God. He's dead, isn't he?" Margaret Robinson began to cry hysterically.

"No, No, Mrs. Robinson. I didn't mean to startle you." Matthews moved inside the door and ran a hand over his thinning hair. He smiled again to reassure her. "Can we go sit down somewhere, maybe the living room or den?"

"Oh, yes... yes, of course. You scared me silly." Margaret struggled to regain her composure. She fumbled in a pocket and found a tissue with which she mopped her eyes and wiped her nose. "I wasn't expecting anyone to show up. The officer said I'd be called if there was any news, and I haven't heard a word for over a week now—not since I called the night he didn't come home. When I saw you at the door, I just knew you were bringing me bad news."

Leading the way into her living room, Margaret indicated the policeman should be seated. "I talked with Mr.

Vickers from Cybertech, my husband's boss, and he said all of this was so unlike Bill. Have you found my husband? Is there any news?"

"Actually, we haven't found out very much, ma'am," Matthews began as he sank into the overstuffed couch. He shifted slightly to relieve the pressure from his thirty-eight revolver, which was digging into his side. "We did find his car parked in long-term parking at the airport. The car was fine, ma'am. Nothing out of place; no sign of foul play. It's been there collecting dust for about ten to twelve days."

"Yes, he left two weeks ago Monday, and he was due back at the end of that week. We were supposed to go to my uncle's retirement party when he got home. He's always come home before," she added in a soft voice and again fished the soggy tissue out of her pocket.

"We checked with the airlines—American Airlines— in case you didn't know, Mrs. Robinson," Matthews quickly explained, hoping to stave off another bout of sobbing. "His luggage is at the airport, so we know he checked in at the Houston terminal."

"His luggage is here?" Margaret looked confused. "So where is he? He didn't just get off the plane in mid-air. Did the plane stop somewhere?"

"No, ma'am. It was a direct flight, Houston to LAX."

"Well, where is he? Did something happen to him here at the airport?" Once again, tears began to run down her cheeks and she sobbed quietly. Matthews noted that her eyes were puffy and red from continual crying or, possibly, from lack of sleep.

He had guessed right. Margaret was exhausted. She

had been sleeping sporadically, spending the murky hours pacing back and forth through dimly lit rooms. Endless cups of black coffee had been consumed as she flipped through television channels until most had gone off the air at two A.M.

Matthews waited patiently until her sobs subsided. "We've sent an inquiry to Houston airport security for a copy of the passenger manifest, to make sure he was on that plane; however, we probably won't have anything back from them until sometime later this week."

"That long! But what if he's hurt? What if he's in the hospital?"

"We checked that possibility but nothing has turned up so far. We'll be in touch if anything develops. Matthews got up and headed for the door, trailed by Margaret who was still sniffling. "Thank you, Mr. Matthews. I want you to know I do appreciate you coming out here." Just before he got to the door, Margaret tugged at Matthews' sleeve. "Please call me. Please... any time at all."

"Yes, ma'am. We have your number."

Before Matthews crawled into his car he surveyed the house. It was the typical white bungalow, he noted—similar to others in Anaheim—with outdoor lighting, a pocket-sized yard and a one-car garage. Neatly kept up, he thought. Almost identical houses on each side. Fair neighborhood. Well-lit streets.

His wife appeared to be devoted to him Matthews reflected. Wonder how he feels about her? Wonder if something bad really has happened to him... here or back in Houston? "Well, a few more days ought to tell the whole story, one way or the other," he said to himself. As the brown four-door sedan pulled away from the curb, Simon and Garfunkel could be heard chanting faintly above the slipping fan belt, *"So, here's to you, Mrs. Robinson…"*

As Mike Nolan entered the President's office at Cybertech, he was met by a bellow from its CEO, Alexander Vickers.

"We've finally found out why Bill Robinson is missing," Vickers stated to Nolan, Cybertech's Vice President. "There is also a large sum of money missing—well not missing—taken. My God! How could someone get to us this way?"

Vickers slammed his fist down on his desk. On the wall behind the desk hung a large charcoal drawing of stampeding elephants, and the room with its dark mahogany paneling and deep maroon carpet exuded a sense of wealth and power.

"What are you saying exactly," Nolan looked puzzled. He was a small man, just over five foot tall. Highly polished shoes, a paisley cravat and neatly creased trousers gave him a dapper appearance.

"I'm not sure what I'm saying. Apparently, and we're still checking—we've hired an outside auditing agency—but our new money management computer program has revealed that a small percentage of every employee's paycheck has been removed for the last three years and paid into an account for several fictitious employees at our various locations. In addition, it appears that fairly large sums of money were diverted into another account under the guise of fees paid to consultants. We're almost certain that Robinson set up these accounts for himself. He could do this because of how the programs were installed and because of his expertise in that area. As you know, he wrote many of our programs."

"Bill Robinson. I find that hard to believe. He was one of our best." Nolan ran his hand through his thinning brown hair, took a handkerchief out of his breast pocket and began to clean rimless glasses. His nearly colorless hazel eyes peered back at Vickers.

"Nevertheless, his position in this company gave him access to records to do this. Also, the deposits to the fake employees and consultant fees stopped at the time of Robinson's disappearance." Vickers shook his head. "Don't you think that's quite a coincidence?"

Vickers moved to the windows which made up one entire wall of his office and drummed his fingers on the glass. In the distance he could see the haze over the ocean and a gull lazily soaring above the waves. At fifty-two, he was no longer thin. Too much bourbon and heavy business luncheons had thickened his waist to where the expensive suit could not camouflage his excesses. His heavy, prematurely white hair was combed straight back from his forehead, emphasizing piercing black eyes and a prominent nose. He was the type of man who was always addressed as Mr. Vickers or, occasionally, Alexander—

never casually by nicknames such as Alex or Vick.

Nolan shook his head. "I can't believe it. And no one had any inkling of this? Where did the money go?"

"The money was deposited into the Southern Pacific Bank under the account name of Anthony Stevens. As far as we can tell there is no Anthony Stevens. It's merely a false name used to set up the account. We checked with the bank this morning, and the account was closed right after Robinson didn't return home. He was one smart S.O.B."

"Well, what are we talking about here? How much did he take?"

"I'm not sure. At least seven and a half million. Probably more. He's had years to get at us." Vickers gritted his teeth and shook his head in disbelief. "The people from the auditing agency are working overtime on it, and I should have a fairly accurate report in a few days."

Nolan was stunned by the amount of money Vickers had mentioned. Finally he sputtered. "Are we really talking about Bill Robinson—the Bill Robinson who always gets his reports in on time, who belongs to Rotary and the Lions Club?"

"I know. I know," Vickers agreed, "but that's what threw us off. He was the ideal employee, so no one questioned what he did. If we hadn't instituted that new program, Corporate Finance 2000, which as one of its many functions checks and rechecks all disbursements, we might never have found out. Just on a whim since he has disappeared, I decided to have the auditors check out his work, and this is what turned up."

"So are you saying that's why he's gone?" Nolan asked.

"Probably so. What other reason could there be?" With

his background in programming, he would have known the capability of Corporate Finance 2000 and understood the consequences for him if he stayed. That's why we hired him. He had all of that computer training from the military, and he was good. You know we relied on him not only to write new programs for us here at headquarters, but we sent him out as our number one troubleshooter to our other seventeen branches and to companies who wished to purchase our services or had problems with our product. God only knows if he was also ripping off our clients." Vickers sighed loudly and sat back at his desk. For a few moments neither man spoke. Outside the office a telephone rang, and a female voice could be heard answering it. When there was no interruption, Nolan surmised that Vickers had instructed his secretary that he wanted no calls from anyone.

"You've spoken to the police?" Nolan finally asked.

"Yes, and so has his wife. However, there's not much they can go on, and this isn't the equivalent of a Hillside Strangler case, so it isn't of top importance to them. Also, the police still think it's just a missing person situation, possibly a domestic problem."

"Who else knows about this—the missing money?" Nolan interjected quickly. "Are we facing publicity?"

"No one, but that's a good point. It's just you, me and the auditors. We haven't even mentioned the missing funds to the police." Vickers straightened some papers on his desk and glanced sharply at Nolan. "And let's keep it that way, Mike. Not a word to anyone. I certainly don't want this to get out to the public and tarnish our image, nor do I want board members unduly alarmed."

"What about the employees," Nolan asked. "They certainly couldn't be too happy to learn they've been short changed on their pay. It makes us look awfully sloppy—stupid even—that we don't check out payroll more carefully. Plus they might expect the corporation to replace what Robinson took. We might be legally liable to do just that."

"You could be right. We'll need to check that issue out, but quietly." Vickers stressed the word quietly. "There are all sorts of problems involved in this mess."

Getting up and moving to the window again, Vickers sighed audibly. "If we want more done about this situation, I guess we're going to have to hire our own person and foot the bill." He turned back to face Nolan. "I simply won't let Robinson get away with this. Do you hear me? I don't care what it costs."

"Well, I know a guy that used to go to I. U. with me back in Indiana. He was a criminology major, has written a couple of books on the subject of white collar theft and teaches now at Pepperdine," Nolan began. "I remember that he was occasionally called in by the police or some firm when theft was suspected. If we paid him enough, he might be willing to ask for some time out of the classroom and look into this for us."

"With a great deal of discretion!" Vickers emphasized. "A great deal of discretion."

"Definitely! Definitely!"

"O. K., Mike," Vickers replied after mulling the idea over for a few minutes. "I want to get Robinson—the bastard. I don't like anyone making a fool of me. What's the name of this guy you want to bring in?"

"Charles Dylan. Why don't I contact him, explain our problem and see if he is willing to come in and at least talk with us. You can decide then if he's the man for the job." Nolan walked to the door, still shaking his head. Bill Robinson a thief; it didn't seem possible.

The days stretched lazily into one another—days of both contemplation and planning for Todd. He acquired a tan during the morning hours, to avoid Tina who slept until around noon, established his cover as a writer by "working" afternoons and usually moved away from the beach house mainly late in the evening or at night. Frequently, he and Rhonda would take a drive up the coast after she came home from work. He liked Rhonda because she had an alert mind. She also had a wry sense of humor and was not nearly as annoying as Tina. Besides, he knew the appearance of dating Rhonda helped with his cover as a virile young author hoping to cash in on a best seller. However, he was careful to take Tina to dinner occasionally and often spent an hour or so with her, lazily sipping a beer on the deck or making up a foursome at gin rummy prior to her heading out for her hostess job. He certainly did not want Tina to feel that he was neglecting her obvious charms; besides that, she kept him aware of anyone making inquiries about his occupation and the extent of progress on his book.

During these few summer months, he carefully reassessed his next move. So far, his prudent planning had paid off. Evaluating his finances, he found that things were better than he had hoped. Taking in all of the deposits from a previous scam and his funds from Cybertech, plus interest, he saw that he had accumulated just over ten million dollars. A good start but not enough. He had hoped to get at least another million from Cybertech before having to disappear. However, the forthcoming implementation of program CF 2000 had forced him to move up the timetable of his plans. Fortunately, he always planned ahead; he had always planned ahead, trying to anticipate every move he would need to make. It was the unexpected—like Tina—that caused him problems.

Even when he was in the Air Force, he had tried to be prepared for any eventuality. The insurance scam he had set up during those years had been a good one what with the Vietnam War and so many men being sent overseas. No one suspected nor had any airman complained about the "insurance policy" premium he deducted from each man's monthly pay and that was automatically deposited to a fake bank account which he had opened at a local savings and loan and then moved to Europe. Unfortunately, he could only do this for Air Force personnel going overseas to the Southeast Asia area, and the premiums were small—just $6.13 per month. Still, the two years he had been able to deduct that amount had provided him with a little over $867,000. Again, not nearly enough, but it had showed him what he had thought for a long time. It was so easy, so very easy. People never seemed to pay attention to their finances, especially if what was deducted was a small amount. And, apparently, the men involved had merely assumed, as he had thought they would, that it was legitimate protection for their families in case they were killed. He had found out, then, just how unsuspecting and gullible people could be.

That little venture had also taught him something else extremely important. When the money had started rolling into the fake account, he had foolishly bought a flashy Camaro convertible and an expensive Hi-Fi set. He learned not to do this, not to be ostentatious but rather to maintain as much anonymity as possible. Sergeant Ravens, who worked with him in the personnel section had become suspicious.

"Where'd a fellow like you get money for these fancy wheels," he had asked as Todd gave him a lift into town one Friday night.

Todd had lied, saying that his dad had died, leaving a large insurance policy, and his mother had sent him some of the money.

"Your dad died? When? I didn't hear of it until now."

Todd explained that his last leave had been used to attend his father's funeral. He thought the sergeant had heard about the death.

But Ravens would not let the matter of the new auto drop. Even though the sergeant often accompanied him off the base and occasionally borrowed the Camaro, Ravens continued to appear skeptical of the explanation of inherited money. Finally, Todd had taken care of that little problem. The sergeant wasn't around long to doubt him, and Todd had learned to be much less conspicuous with his spending—overly frugal even. At Cybertech, both

Margaret and his co-workers thought that, as good old Bill Robinson, he was just one of the company' average wage earners.

Cybertech! He could not help smiling with satisfaction as he thought of it. His years at the corporation had provided him with considerably more wealth than the military. He had begun by skimming a portion of each employees' pay check—an additional eighty-six cents which supposedly was going to medical coverage. The pittance merely was sidetracked by the computer program, which he had instigated, into other false accounts located across the country. At first, he had felt a tiny twinge of guilt at taking money from his fellow co-workers; then he reasoned that the eighty-six cents was so small it did no real harm. In addition, he had set up false charges from several consultant firms as Cybertech used a myriad of these for various services. That theft brought in a hefty sum and didn't bother him at all. Big business took advantage of the working man, he thought, and this merely helped even the odds. He had been actively accumulating for a little over five years when the unexpected happened—CF 2000. He had actively worked on that project, had untangled several problems in its operation but had thought it would be sold to other companies, not used by Cybertech. He knew once it was implemented in the home office, his extra curricular activities would be discovered.

Now, he was ready to move on. He figured that six months of vanishing from the corporate sector would lead any investigation to a dead end. Bill Robinson had simply ceased to exist —- actually had never existed. Todd Walker could settle in, relax and wait.

Tfter several extended telephone conversations with both Nolan and Vickers, Dylan accepted the challenge to attempt to locate the missing Bill Robinson and the missing millions. He was at Cybertech's office before nine A.M. and was ushered into Vickers' office by a flustered secretary who thought she had forgotten to list an early appointment on Vicker's calendar. Dylan explained to her that he was always an early riser, had been since his stint in the Marine Corps, and that she had not been remiss in her scheduling of appointments.

"Thanks, I will have a cup of coffee," he said, smiling graciously at the secretary.

She scurried out and returned in a few minutes with a small silver tray on which were set a carafe, sugar and creamer and cup and saucer, all Dylan noted in what his wife Barbara would term "guest" China.

"Nice," he thought. "Not your usual styrofoam cup and paper napkin." He took the coffee that the secretary handed him, declined the proffered cream and sugar and made himself comfortable on the tan leather sofa which was placed diagonally across a corner of the expansive room.

Even though it seemed the whole world had long hair, Dylan wore his in a flattop—-a holdover from the Corps and the couple of years he had spent with the F.B.I. Barbara said it made him look like an escaped convict from a fifties movie. She had urged him to wear a suit, but he had opted for a navy blazer, a rather somber tie with just a hint of red, and light gray slacks. Deep set piercing blue eyes under thick brows topped a hawk-like nose, and after drinking his coffee he paced restlessly about the office, moving occasionally to peer out the windows at the panorama below. Dylan was not known for his patience, never had been, and he thought waiting for anyone a complete waste of his time. Turning to greet the two Cybertech executives as they entered the office, his six feet seemed to dwarf both Nolan and Vickers.

"The first thing I'd better do," Dylan told the two men, after they had thoroughly discussed the problem of the missing man and the missing millions, is find out what I can in Houston. After all, we know Robinson checked in at that airport. Maybe someone will remember him or remember seeing him leave with someone. If nothing pans out there, I'll probably need to check Miami, Chicago, Boston and New York—the other places he was on this last trip. It won't be an easy job. I will be gone several days at least."

"That's not a problem," Vickers said as the men shook hands. "I want this guy found. No one makes a fool of me."

"But someone has," Dylan thought as he left the building. "Someone who may not be a fool himself."

Before leaving for Houston Dylan picked up a copy of the passenger manifest from flight 409 which the L.A. police had requested when they were looking into Robinson's disappearance. On the flight to Houston, Dylan spent his time reviewing the manifest and quickly eliminating families who had been on the plane. He would concentrate his effort on the single males. When he arrived in Houston, Dylan surveyed the airport looking for the most likely place a businessman would spend time waiting for his flight. The "Prop Wash" was the typical between-planes watering hole located in the vicinity of the gates to attract both incoming and outgoing passengers. The lighting was dim, the music soft and the drink prices high. As he settled on a red vinyl bar stool, Dylan noted that the clientele was chiefly men in business suits with briefcases nestled beside them and a sprinkling of women at the few tables near the door. In general the patrons appeared relaxed even as they frequently checked their watches.

"Vodka on the rocks," Dylan told the bartender, a solidly built man with graying hair and a tag on his shirt which proclaimed to the world that his name was Dan. His drink appeared instantaneously as the man hurried to greet another customer. Dylan sipped his drink and waited patiently.

"Flight 409 to Los Angeles now boarding," the announcement intruded on a chorus crooning, "Come fly with me; let's fly away..." Almost as one body the men and women gathered their belongings and headed for the gate to flight 409, leaving Dylan and three other men as the sole occupants of the bar. Two waitresses busily emptied ashtrays and cleared tables. Dylan ordered another vodka and fumbled in his jacket pocket for a copy of Bill Robinson's I.D. photo which was provided to all Cybertech employees. It was a poor copy, but he hoped it would suffice.

"I know you see a million faces every year, but I'm trying to locate this man," Dylan began as the bartender placed the new drink in front of him. "Take a look, please. Something might ring a bell with you."

"Nope, can't place him," Dan remarked after glancing at the photo. "Looks like many of the guys I see going through this place. What's he done?"

"Nothing that I'm aware of. He's just your average business man. But he disappeared, after checking in for his flight a few weeks ago. The police have found nothing. His employer, a big company in L.A., hired me to try and find out what happened. He's married, and, of course, his wife is frantic."

"Too bad," Dan replied, but he lingered a moment longer. "Let me get Donna Sue over here for you. She chats with the customers more than I do—gets her some good tips sometimes." He called to one of the waitresses, a slim redhead with a ready smile.

"What? What?" she asked in a raspy voice as she joined Dylan and Dan. "I'm busy; we'll have another plane load soon, and I need to get these tables cleared."

"Look at this picture, will ya? This guy needs to know if we've ever seen him. He's gone missing."

"Well," Donna Sue examined Robinson's photo carefully. "He's pretty ordinary looking.... .but, you know, he could be that guy we bought the drink for."

"What guy?" Dan queried.

"Remember, there was this guy a couple weeks ago who stopped here and ordered the Rusty Nail. Remember, we didn't have any Drambuie, so you couldn't make him one. So, like we say, if we can't provide your request, we'll buy you a free one."

"Oh, yeah, I do remember that," the bartender replied. "Are you sure this is the guy?"

"No," Donna Sue shot back, "but it sort of looks like him. I remember he was talking with another guy 'cause that guy said something to the effect that he should have ordered a Rusty Nail, and he would also have gotten a free drink."

"Do you remember him leaving," Dylan interjected. "Did the other man leave with him?"

"Can't say. I know they talked for quite a spell." She cocked her head to one side and frowned. "Nope! That's the best I can do." She handed the photo back to Dylan, flashed him a smile and returned to her cleaning up chores.

"Hope that helps," Dan added.

"You've been a big help," Dylan replied as he finished

the last of his vodka and left a tip on the counter.

"Oh, wait," Donna Sue called as Dylan got off the bar stool. "I do remember something else. If that is the guy you're looking for, he left me a two dollar bill. You know you don't see many of them. Sorta stuck in my mind."

"This is for you, Donna Sue," Dylan said smiling. He handed the girl a ten and headed for the door.

You certainly earned it, Dylan thought as he sauntered toward short-term parking. Probably a lot of people drink Rusty Nails; however, it obviously was not a popular drink here or the bar would have stocked Drambuie. But the two-dollar bill, that was extremely interesting; not many people carried two-dollar bills.

Dylan picked up his rental car and headed back to his room at the Holiday Inn. As he changed into slacks and a polo shirt, he continued mulling over the problem. Why would anyone use two-dollar bills if he were deliberately running? Is he that confident that he won't be found? Obviously, the two-dollar bill was rare enough that Donna Sue remembered it. Was that merely a coincidence or did Robinson frequently use two-dollar bills? It didn't seem to make sense to Dylan. And the other guy, how does he come into all of this? Maybe he was just a fellow traveler, or maybe he and Robinson were in this scam together.

Dylan decided to go down to the restaurant for a quick dinner. The place was nearly empty, and the hostess gave him his choice of booths. He selected one near a window but found that the view was chiefly of the motel parking lot and the ubiquitous ivy ground cover with a few bushes and a scraggly pine. Shortly a harried mother with three children came in, and Dylan was treated to some heated squabbling as the kids vied for the woman's attention. His pork chops were overdone, the mixed vegetables had been as tasteless as the cardboard box from which they apparently came, and the coffee was only lukewarm. He contemplated getting a beer in the bar but decided it would be best to turn in early. He had a busy day planned for tomorrow.

The next morning he visited the Houston companies on Robinson's Cybertech itinerary and learned that Robinson had been at each place. No one had noticed anything out of the ordinary about the man and were baffled by his failure to return home. His disappearance had to occur at the Houston airport or the one in L.A. Dylan concluded. But which one?

Returning to L.A., Dylan began the arduous job of tracking down the forty plus businessmen who had been on flight 409. It was a tedious task. After several days he gave up the search, leaving five names which he could neither track down nor verify that they had been on the flight. Next, he decided to talk with Margaret Robinson, both for background information and to try to determine if she were involved in the scheme.

"**M**rs. Robinson, I'm Charles Dylan. A. A. Cybertech has retained me to investigate the disappearance of your husband." He noted Margaret's disheveled appearance and the untidy look of the house as she led him into the living room. Newspapers were scattered on the sofa and floor, and a sprinkling of unwashed coffee cups littered the end tables. It reminded him of other homes he had visited when a death had been involved, as though those left behind simply couldn't cope with the everyday chores involved in living.

"The place is a mess. I just don't seem to have the energy to clean it up after I come home from work," Margaret explained, looking numbly around the cluttered room. "And the neighbors have been in..." Her words drifted off.

"I'm sure this has been a great shock to you." Dylan eased into the proffered wing chair which was upholstered with a muted plaid pattern. He noted the charcoal drawings of famous architecture over the sofa, their gold frames adding a touch of color to the pale green walls. As in many ranch houses of the time, the wall-to-wall carpet was the usual dull beige color which "went with everything."

"You've heard nothing at all from Mr. Robinson since he didn't come home?"

"No, and I won't. He's dead. I know it." Margaret stated flatly, a vacant look in her eyes.

"Well, I wouldn't be too hasty, if I were you. Perhaps I could get some information that would enable us to find out what really happened."

"Of course, whatever I can do. I want to know. I've just got to know. You can understand that, can't you? Can't you?"

"Certainly," Dylan answered soothingly, "and I'm going to try to get you an answer."

"Oh, I'm sorry if I was sharp. It's just that I'm so worried. What can I tell you?" She settled onto the thin cushions of the sofa, upholstered in a rough material similar to burlap and nearly the color of the carpet. Quickly, Margaret pushed two brightly flowered pillows into one corner.

"Well, has Mr. Robinson... let's just call him Bill. Is that all right?"

"Oh, sure. Everyone always calls him Bill."

"Well, has Bill ever done this before, not come home for a period of time?"

"Oh, no!" Margaret exclaimed, a bewildered look on her face. "He even calls if he thinks he'll be late."

"Would he have gone to see some family member, his parents, brothers, sisters?"

"He doesn't have any family. I remember when we got married; just my family was at the ceremony. He was an only child..."

"What about his parents?" Dylan interjected.

"Oh, his parents both died before he went into the military. He is all alone, except for me."

"He was in the military—the Army?"

"No, the Air Force. He was in for quite a long time, I think." Suddenly the interview was interrupted by the loud ringing of a telephone. Margaret excused herself and left the room.

The military, Dylan mused. That is a piece of news. Was that in his Cybertech personnel file? Dylan didn't think he had overlooked the fact. When Margaret failed to reappear, and he could hear the murmur of her continuing conversation, he got up and wandered into a small adjoining room which appeared to be an office. Stark white walls were covered with a myriad of framed photos and certificates showing Margaret and Bill at various company functions and acknowledging Bill's contribution to volunteerism in several civic organizations. On a cluttered desk was an old pipe and an open package of tobacco. Dylan sniffed the aroma. Obviously a blend—expensive, perhaps rather special, Dylan thought. He'd have to check that out at a tobacco shop. He put a small amount into his coat pocket.

A large photo over one bookcase showed a younger Bill and Margaret. The traditional wedding picture, Dylan noted, and suddenly stopped. No military mementoes. No "love me" wall, as former military referred to dens rife with framed U.S. flags, plaques from numerous assignments and certificates of appreciation. That's odd.

"Oh, I'm so sorry," Margaret apologized, coming in from the living room. "It was someone from church. Where were we?"

"You were telling me about his military career," Dylan replied as they resettled themselves in the living room.

"Well, I really don't know too much about it. He was in during the Vietnam War, but I don't think he went. He never talked about it, like a lot of men, I suppose. I didn't ask him much either. I didn't want to push it."

"Do you know where his copy of his discharge records are, or did he keep any photos of the places he had been stationed?"

"Not that I've seen. I think he was stationed up in Colorado, in Denver. He didn't have much in the way of personal stuff, just some bits and pieces of furniture, which I guess he bought when he left the Air Force."

"And he never told you if he flew planes or what his job was in the service?" Dylan was incredulous that Margaret could have married this man—apparently a total stranger—and lived with him several years without knowing anything about him.

"No, I think he did things with computers, in the payroll section or the section that dealt with hiring the men."

"Is that how he got his job with A. A. Cybertech—because of his knowledge of computer work?"

"I guess so. I met him after he'd been there a while."

"Did you work there also, Mrs. Robinson?"

"No, I met Bill at church. One of his fellow employees, my uncle actually, brought him to a church picnic. It was almost love at first sight for me. I don't know about what Bill thought, but for me..."

"Did Bill have any special interests or hobbies—fishing, golf, furniture refinishing—anything that he did in his leisure time?" Dylan wanted to keep her focused on his questions.

"Not really. He didn't have too much leisure time. He was on business trips all over the country a couple of weeks each month." Margaret pushed her hair back from her face and leaned forward in her chair. "I'm trying to be helpful, Mr. Dylan. I just can't seem to think straight."

"Take your time, Mrs. Robinson. I'm in no hurry, and anything you can tell me about your husband's habits or interests may help us solve this mystery."

Margaret smiled slightly and shrugged. "I can't think of anything out of the ordinary. Bill read a great deal whenever he had a spare moment at home. In fact, he read constantly, and he was interested in art. I remember him telling me several times that he had visited museums around the country; he always said that if he was rich, he'd buy great art. But I was never much interested in that. I couldn't understand a lot of it—you know—the modern stuff. It just looked like kid's finger painting to me with all those colors just splashed across a canvas... "

"Any particular type of reading material?" Dylan couldn't seem to stop her rambling.

"As I recall mostly history and travel books, especially books on travel. I don't read much myself, but, as I said, Bill would read almost anything. He had a wide range of interests. In fact I used to tell him that he'd read the labels on cans if that was all there was."

Margaret paused, her thoughts drifting away again. Dylan shifted in his chair and waited. She was listless, wilted, like a hothouse blossom that lacked proper watering. He hated to bring up any unpleasant subject as she seemed so fragile. However, he needed all the information he could get.

"Were there..." Dylan hesitated, "I don't mean to be offensive, but I have to ask this question. Were there any problems in the marriage?"

Astonished, Margaret gave an emphatic reply. "No! Definitely not. We are very happy, very happy. Bill is a great husband. He is considerate, loving..." She sputtered to a stop. "You don't know what you're asking. Why, just a couple of months ago he surprised me with a gorgeous string of pearls—not the cheap kind—South Sea island pearls."

"An anniversary or birthday gift?" Dylan asked politely.

"No, but that's what I'm telling you. That just shows you what kind of man Bill is. Bill always is home if he's not on a business trip. He's a good provider. Everyone likes him. And, if you're suggesting that he is involved with another woman, that's completely out of the question. I would know if there was anything wrong."

"I'm sure you would." Dylan smiled reassuringly and got off the subject. How many times in his criminology interviews had he heard wives, parents, employers make that same statement? Most people did not know there was anything wrong, as Margaret put it, until some unexpected problem arose. Or, as in Bill Robinson's case, until someone disappeared or some crime had been committed. However, he immediately switched his line of questioning. He knew Margaret Robinson was going to have enough to think about later on without his raising the specter of marital infidelity.

"What type of work do you do, Mrs. Robinson?"

"I'm a secretary with a real estate agency."

"And no financial problems that you know of?"

"No, we aren't rich, of course, but we always pay our

bills and manage to save a little money. Just last year, Bill got a large bonus from the company and we paid off the mortgage on the house. I guess you could say that put us in pretty good financial shape."

"Pretty good financial shape was an understatement," Dylan thought.

"What did Bill's co-workers think about him getting this nice bonus?"

"Oh, I'm not sure they knew. Bill said not to mention it as it would make our friends feel bad. I think it came as a complete surprise to him also."

"I'll just bet it did," Dylan mused to himself, thinking of the amount Vickers had said was stolen. Obviously Robinson could well afford to pay off the mortgage on their home and buy the expensive pearls with the money he had taken from Cybertech. But why a surprise gift? Was Robinson the type who would indulge in surprises or had he actually felt guilty about his upcoming plans to abandon his wife? Did Robinson have the type of personality that included feelings of guilt?

Momentarily Dylan stopped his questions and stared at Margaret Robinson. Without lipstick, her mouth appeared too small, and her eyes seemed overly large. Evidently she had not fixed her hair since coming from work as the brown curls hung limply down her back. Not a pretty face—pleasant might be a better description— but it had an open, innocent look. Could she be so naive, so trusting of her husband? Had Robinson been able to maintain two completely separate lives without her noticing anything at all?

"Well, Mrs. Robinson, you've been very helpful. I think

that's all I need at the moment." Dylan got up and moved toward the door.

"You'll find him, won't you Mr. Dylan? You'll get him back here, won't you?"

"I'll certainly do my best." But as Dylan got into his car, he thought, "but I won't be bringing him home, Margaret."

Dylan began the laborious task of interviewing Robinson's co-workers at Cybertech, although there would be no mention of the missing funds. A memo had been sent out indicating that since the police had not been able to locate Bill Robinson, the company was doing its own investigation and would appreciate cooperation from all employees if they were contacted by a Mr. Charles Dylan. Dylan first chatted with Mrs. Ruth Davis, the secretary Robinson shared with another co-worker. She was middle-aged, with tightly curled hair, and dressed in an appropriate business suit.

"Mrs. Davis, the company feels that it should do something to try and find out what happened to Bill Robinson, for Mrs. Robinson's sake as well as the company's.'

"I do hope they find him. He was such a nice man."

"You knew him well?"

"No, only as his secretary, but he was always so nice to work with. He was never impatient nor rude to me. You know how some people are. They expect miracles."

"Did he say anything... did he mention anything

odd or any concerns he might have had before he left on his trip?"

"No, I made the airplane and hotel reservations as I always did. He expected to be back for Jim Dawson's retirement party." Ruth Davis frowned slightly, trying to remember if she had forgotten anything.

"Did you talk with him at all while he was gone?"

"Once. He called from St. Louis needing some information, just before he was to go on to Houston. I mailed the information to him in Houston."

Dylan could see that Mrs. Davis was of no help. She had worked closely with Robinson for several years; yet, like Margaret Robinson, she knew almost nothing about the man—certainly nothing of a personal nature. He needed to talk with a couple of other co-workers. The first one he chose was Joe Stone.

Stone shook hands with Dylan and ushered him to a chair in the small cubicle which served as his office. He appeared to be about the same age as Bill Robinson, but there the resemblance ended. Stone had bright red hair which curled in a mat around his head. His face was heavily freckled, and he had a pronounced lisp which no one had bothered to mention to Dylan.

"Mr. Stone, I understand from what Margaret Robinson said that you and your wife, Ann, were close friends with her and Bill."

"We are. I always think of Bill Robinson as thomeone great." Stone spoke of Robinson in the present tense. "We thee a great deal of them. We go to the thame church, and Bill and I are in Rotary together."

In the beginning the lisp threw Dylan off a bit. He

could see why Stone had gone into programming. He would not have to meet the public on a daily basis and be embarrassed by his speech problem.

"Can you tell me anything about him... his habits... any quirks? This is not just idle curiosity; I'm hoping something may be a lead to why he is missing."

"No. He ith an ordinary guy, like me. Always doth a great job, one of the best programmerth the place has. That was hith life—computer programming." Stone lit a cigarette and offered one to Dylan. Dylan declined.

"Nothing unusual about his private life that you know of?"

"No. He and Margaret are not having any trouble that I know of. Bill ith attentive, caring. He goes out of hith way to make thertain Margaret ith happy."

"No hobbies, that you can remember?"

Stone thought for a few minutes. "No. He plays golf occasionally but not very well. I think he just does it becauth it ith expected."

"Nothing unusual at all," Dylan persisted.

"Welllll," Dylan could see that Stone was at a loss to come up with an answer. "He does thmoke some funny kind of tobacco. It hath a very strong but pleasant thmell. And now and then he would give my kidth two-dollar bills. Thaid they were lucky—brings luck to the giver and the receiver. My kidth adore him."

Dylan thanked Stone for his help, and it might be quite a bit of help. While he knew about the tobacco from his visit to Margaret Robinson, the information on the two-dollar bills was especially interesting. He spoke with several other of Robinson's co-workers, but the story was always the same. Bill Robinson was a saint—a real nice guy, quiet, good worker, good neighbor, never any trouble. "He's just too good to be real," Dylan thought. It appeared that he was the type it would be hard to trace. No outstanding physical features or personal habits. Just a blank when it came to identity. A lot of people knew him and liked him. Yet, they could hardly describe him. Either this was the true Bill Robinson or this man had gone out of his way to be like a mirage. "You think you see him, but you only see his shadow," Dylan laughed, shaking his head.

The last person Dylan interviewed was Margaret's uncle, Jim Dawson, the recently retired supervisor of Bill Robinson. Dylan had called Dawson earlier and explained why he wanted to talk with him. He found Dawson in his office on Euclid Street. The place smelled of new paint and carpet. Dawson, a big, blustery man of around fifty-five was busily unpacking boxes, and the office was strewn with files and reference books.

"Just getting set up," Dawson said after shaking hands. "Still don't have my name on the door. Sign painter will be here tomorrow."

"I was told you had retired," Dylan said.

"I am retired from Cybertech. Felt I had to get out on my own. I've made a lot of contacts, and I wanted to try my hand at consulting work. Figure I'll work another ten years and then retire for good. The wife and I would like to travel in Europe for a spell."

Dawson scraped some files off a chair, indicated that Dylan should have a seat and sat himself on the corner of his desk, a rather ostentatious piece of furniture made of cherry wood. From the sun streaming through the window, Dylan noted dust particles hanging in the air.

"Still no trace of Bill?" Dawson asked.

"No, nothing so far. I've checked in Houston, but no one saw anything unusual at the airport."

"Just can't believe this," Dawson continued. "I expected him to be at my retirement bash, and we had a date set up to play golf the next day."

"You were his boss, weren't you," Dylan inquired, although he already had this information.

"Yep. He worked for me, although I wasn't really a 'boss' as you put it, for seven years. He pretty much worked on his own these past few years as he had to travel quite a bit for us."

"But you were close to him; you knew him fairly well?"

"Hell, yes! I'm the one who introduced him to Margaret, my niece. I wouldn't have done that—wouldn't have brought him into the family—if I hadn't known the guy well."

"I'm certain you wouldn't, Mr. Dawson." Dylan noticed Dawson's hands, big and strong with a few liver spots already beginning to show. Dawson's breath reeked of peppermint, bringing to Dylan's attention the large glass container of mints set atop a computer printer which took up most of one corner of the office.

"I saw this guy at least six days a week," Dawson continued. "We were in meetings regularly."

"So you could definitely identify him?" Dylan interrupted.

"Definitely!" Dawson emphasized the word. "We went to the same church; my wife and I had them to dinner often and were invited to their home. Margaret's a great cook, incidentally—does a fantastic pot roast. Then, we were together at the office all the time unless he was out of town. My wife and I really thought of him as our nephew. She always commented on how good looking he was, although I guess women are more attuned to that sort of thing. But, as I said, we were very close to Bill."

Dylan waited a minute, musing on the fact that everyone he had talked with emphasized how well they knew Robinson when no one, obviously, knew him at all. Finally, he asked, "No financial problems that you know of?"

"Not that I know of. Course he didn't discuss things like that with me, and I never asked. He had a good salary from Cybertech—not the top of the line—but a good amount. Bill never seemed to be particularly interested in being a leader. He was just a good, dependable worker. Smart as a whip when it came to computers. But I do know that he and Margaret weren't spendthrifts. They had two cars, but he usually drove the old Capri and let her have the newer Buick."

"Thanks, Mr. Dawson." Dylan got up to leave. This interview had been like the others—basically no help.

"You'll let me know if you learn anything, won't you." Dawson asked. "Margaret is beside herself with fear that he's dead. We've tried to be as much help as possible, but you know how that is?"

"I'm sure Cybertech will keep Mrs. Robinson posted if there is anything new," Dylan replied as he left.

"Yeah. I'm sure they will. They've been great to her so far."

Dylan wondered if Cybertech would continue to be

supportive to Margaret if they were unable to recover the missing funds. And speaking of the funds, Dylan thought it was interesting that Dawson had left the firm just as Robinson disappeared—with all that money. Could it be that Robinson and Dawson had conspired to work this scheme? It must have taken some financial backing to set up Dawson's consulting business.

And what of Margaret? She appeared so innocent, but was she guilty of complicity? If she were the true innocent, would Vickers eventually tell Margaret that her husband had taken the money? If she were to be told, Cybertech would have to do it. It was not his job to tell Margaret her husband was a thief.

Having received no significant help from his interviews at Cybertech, Dylan decided he had better try to track down Robinson's military record. He had been surprised when he checked Robinson's personnel file to learn that no background checks had been done by them. The explanation was that obviously Robinson knew what he was talking about when it came to computers. He had produced a copy of his military discharge, so there was no reason to assume he was lying. Also, computer programmers were in fairly short supply and in great demand when Robinson had been hired, so the company felt fortunate to get him.

Dylan flew to Denver as this was the area Margaret thought Robinson had mentioned to her about his Air Force days. He rented a car and drove from Stapleton Airport to Lowery AFB, which was only ten minutes away. Traffic was heavy but nothing like the snarls of Los Angeles.

"Which way to Base Finance," Dylan asked the security police officer in the Visitor Center at Lowery.

"Just down Mitchell Avenue and then a right on Perimeter Road. You can't miss it," the Sergeant replied as he handed Dylan a visitor pass and a map of the base.

Dark clouds had gathered over the mountains to the west, blotting out the sun, and the damp smell of rain mixed with dust hung in the air. The sweet odor of cottonwoods lingered on the breeze, and the huge trees shaded neatly trimmed lawns around the barracks and commissary. He noted the F4 Phantom on its pedestal, its nose pointed skyward. For just a moment he had a slight feeling of nostalgia, remembering his time on military bases.

Patiently he waited in the austere building which housed the Finance Department until the secretary could locate a Mr. Matthew Stearns, the civilian in charge of disbursements. Stearns was a tall, thin man, apparently nearing retirement age. His graying hair curled around his ears, and black horn-rimmed glasses accented jowls that were beginning to droop. Dylan explained his reasons for being there.

"I have a picture of someone who I believe was stationed here several years ago and who would have worked in this department." Dylan handed a copy of Robinson's wedding photo to Stearns. "Is it possible you might remember him?"

Stearns peered intently at the photo for several minutes. "The men come and go here so frequently, but, yeah, I think I do remember him. I've been here sixteen years, and, you know, after a while all those young guys look alike. But this guy looks like... Josh... I can't seem to remember his last name. Pierce. No, Phelps. No, but it started with a 'P.' Preston. No."

Dylan waited.

"I've got it. Petersen. That was it. Josh Petersen. Good hard working kid. Whiz at computers."

"Petersen," Dylan asked. "Are you certain? This guy's name is Robinson—Bill Robinson."

"Nope. Petersen. I'd bet my pension on it. Check out that plaque on the wall over there. If I remember rightly, he's on it. Made Airman of the Year for this office."

Dylan walked over to the wall. There it was, the name—A1C Joshua N. Petersen, 1970. And the photo, although taken a decade earlier, was a close match to the one Dylan had. Bingo! Dylan thought. Bill Robinson is really Joshua N. Petersen.

"Transferred over to OSI when he made Staff Sergeant. You could check with them. Sure wish he hadn't done that. I could have used him when we had some trouble here."

"Trouble?"

"Well, yeah. I guess I shouldn't be talking about it, but what the hell; it's old hat now." Stearns leaned across the worn counter and continued in a conspiratorial manner. "And they've never solved the crime."

"Crime?" Dylan didn't want to be too pushy.

"Yeah. It was really funny. We only ran across the situation by accident. We had transposed a social security number on one guy's file, and he wasn't getting paid. So when I called up the sheets—you know, computer print-outs—I found the transposed number, but I noticed that quite a few guys were getting deducted for insurance. I didn't think much about it immediately, but a few evenings later it bugged me. Fortunately I had kept the printouts. There was no insurance. It was a scam. One of my guys was taking this supposed insurance money and depositing it in a false bank account. By the time we had discovered all of this, the money had been moved from that account. So we never got any of it back."

"But you caught the culprit?"

"The guy who did it? No. We thought it might have been this other guy who worked with Petersen, but he's dead."

"Dead? He was killed in Vietnam?" Dylan asked.

"Nope. Car crash. Just out of the blue. As I recall it was a convertible, and he was thrown out. He hadn't been drinking or anything. An investigation showed something wrong with the brakes. Just his day to cash out, I guess."

"So Peterson was not in the car?"

"No, he was on some OSI case at the time and was out of town. He and this other guy had been friendly to a degree, not close friends but, you know, friendly enough. I remember that Peterson was very upset that he had loaned the guy his car."

"But you said none of the missing money was ever recovered?" Dylan wanted to make certain he had heard Stearns correctly.

"Nope! Funny thing, though. The stolen money was transferred to another account after his death. Maybe there were two of them scamming. But we couldn't find anything or anyone else, so we just gave up on it."

"Well, it does sound awfully suspicious," Dylan began. "And the guy I'm trying to find has embezzled money from his company. But his name is William T. Robinson. Can you get me some more information on Petersen, and is there some way you could check and see if there were a

William T. Robinson here at Lowery—or in the Air Force during the same time Petersen was here?"

"Take some time, and there must be dozens of William Robinsons who've been in the service," Stearns answered. "But I'll do my best. Stole some money, you say?"

"Yes, quite a bit of money—maybe several million."

"Well, I don't know how much our guy got away with, but it was probably near to a million. The insurance premiums were $6.13 and were taken out of thousands of checks over many months."

"And no one complained about the premiums?" Dylan looked puzzled.

"Nope. Just took the money out of checks for those men who were in Vietnam or Southeast Asia. I imagine most thought it was some kind of insurance protection for their families in case they didn't come back."

"Very shrewd," Dylan commented.

"You can say that again," Stearns replied. "Well, leave me your name and number, and I'll do what I can for you."

The information came quicker than Dylan had hoped. First of all, he learned that the true identity of the photo he had shown Stearns was, indeed, Joshua Nathaniel Petersen, born Duluth, Minnesota in 1950. Petersen had enlisted in the Air Force in 1968 from Minneapolis. Dylan knew his next stop would have to be Minnesota.

Sitting in a window seat as the plane began its descent toward Minneapolis, Dylan could see far below him like a patchwork quilt the varied colors of America's heartland with its fields of ripening grain. A water tower of some small town accented the flat landscape, and a narrow road snaked into the distance.

In Minneapolis, Dylan rented a car for the drive to Duluth. As summer lingered in the fields, the humidity seemed to penetrate the auto's air conditioning. Mosquitoes had attacked Dylan as soon as he left the airport terminal, and he decided Minnesota was not a place he wished ever to reside. However, the expanses of green vegetation along the highway were to his eyes remarkable, compared with the amber grass and muted green of the Eucalyptus trees that were so common to Southern California.

It took Dylan close to four hours to reach Duluth, and it was already late afternoon. He decided to wait until the next day to try and contact Mrs. Karen Petersen, Joshua's mother, as he didn't want to just show up on her doorstep at night. Sitting in the dining room of the Best Western Edgewater West, he tried to fit the pieces of his investigation together.

While he had received some very worthwhile information from the Air Force, he still had a lot of unanswered questions. Was Robinson, as he suspected, really Petersen? Had Petersen been involved in the military insurance scam? Stearns hadn't thought so; in fact he wished Petersen had been there to help clear it up. However, Dylan felt Petersen may have been the culprit and was able to make it appear that his co-worker had been the actual thief. Had the co-worker's death been an accident? He couldn't believe that the Bill Robinson he was looking for could be a murderer, not according to the descriptions given him by Margaret Robinson, Dawson and the Cybertech employees. Dylan was tired of the whole thing. After dinner he decided to take in a movie; tomorrow would be soon enough to get his mind back on the mystery.

Around five A.M. Dylan was awake. He walked out of his room onto the tiny balcony and noticed there was already a ruddy glow in the eastern sky. Nearby he heard the faint song of a loon shattering the early morning stillness. After a hearty breakfast of eggs and pancakes, he set out to locate Karen Petersen.

Huge maple trees formed a canopy across the narrow street on which Karen Petersen lived. Thin shafts of sunlight pierced the dense leaves and, like spotlights in a theater setting, highlighted an occasional colorful blossom in a front garden. The Petersen house was set nearly flush against the street, a somewhat dilapidated building of white clapboard with peeling black shutters and two scruffy bushes on each side of a small porch. Surrounding it were houses of about the same vintage and deterioration. Not too affluent a neighborhood, he thought. It looked like what it was—a part of the city left behind to decay as the suburbs lured the young to the outer edges. I can see why Petersen might join the Air Force he thought. The neighborhood gave him the feeling that most of its inhabitants never had been out of the area but had always wished they could leave.

In response to his knock, a small woman with wiry gray hair opened the door slightly. She smiled hesitantly, a puzzled look on her face. "Yes?"

"Mrs. Petersen," Dylan asked.

"Yes. May I help you?"

"My name is Charles Dylan." Dylan produced his driver's license. "I am an investigator for the A. A. Cybertech Corporation out of Los Angeles. I wonder if you could talk with me for a few minutes. It's about your son, Joshua."

"Josh?" The woman appeared confused. Finally she responded. "Where is he? What's happened to him?"

"That's why I'm here. We're just trying to locate him. Could I come in for a few minutes."

"Well, I guess it will be all right." Karen Petersen said hesitantly, but she finally held the door open.

She led the way down a narrow, dark hall into a cramped kitchen. Dylan noted that the floors were shaky and that the walls had not been newly papered in many years. In fact, the flowered pattern was yellowed and faded, as if the room were in perennial autumn. However, the room was spotless, and he could detect the faint odor of a pine disinfectant. She indicated that he should take a seat in one of the vinyl chairs near a small drop-leaf table.

"I was just having some coffee, Mr....."

"Dylan," Dylan repeated. "Yes, thank you. I'd like a cup."

Karen Petersen poured two large blue mugs of coffee and produced sugar from a cupboard and a bottle of milk from a refrigerator that Dylan thought looked like it had been purchased shortly after the Korean War. "Don't have any cream," she apologized, settling herself on the other side of the table. "Now, Mr. Dylan, how can I help you?"

"I hope you can tell me where your son is presently living," Dylan began.

"I really don't know anything about Josh's whereabouts." Karen Petersen held her hands up as if to show they were empty of any knowledge. "I haven't seen my son since he left here in 1968. I did have a couple of birthday cards with some money and a few lines about his life in the military, but that was the last I actually heard anything about him. That's been nearly ten years ago."

"I have a photo here, Mrs. Petersen. Is this Joshua?"

"He's married?" Karen Petersen held the photo up to get more light from the window. "That's his wife? Isn't she nice looking? Are there any grandchildren?"

"So that is Joshua?" Dylan avoided answering her questions.

"Yes, that's my son, although he's a little heavier, of course. But I can't believe he's married."

"Is there some reason why he wouldn't marry, Mrs. Petersen?"

"Well, he never had much to do with girls. Never dated much. Never went steady as most of the kids did. He was always more interested in his schoolwork and fixing up old cars."

Mrs. Petersen massaged the back of one hand. "Touch of arthritis," she explained and then asked abruptly, "Where did you say he's living now?"

"His home is near L.A. However, he didn't come home from his last business trip. He works for A. A. Cybertech, and that's why I'm here. The company is concerned."

"No one knows where he is? Has something bad happened? You think that, don't you, or you wouldn't be here?"

"Now, now, Mrs. Petersen. We really don't know anything. That's why I'm here. Do you have any idea where Joshua might have gone? Any friends or relatives?"

No, he's an only child, and we had very few relatives. Certainly none that Josh was close to. His father is dead—dead many years now."

"Oh, I'm sorry to hear that. Was it a lengthy illness?" Dylan thought this might account for the poverty of the home.

"No, a car accident. It was winter, cold and very icy. Apparently the brakes went out. That's what the police said. He couldn't stop and slid under a freight train. He was dead when help arrived."

"What a terrible tragedy for you."

"Yes, but as the police said, 'It was just a freak accident.' There's no accounting for accidents."

"How old was Joshua at the time? That must have been extremely difficult for him to adjust to." Dylan could imagine a young boy who suddenly had lost a father.

"Joshua didn't really get along with his father too well.

Of course his dad loved him, really cared a lot about him, and he loved his father, but they seemed to quarrel all the time. You know how it is with fathers and sons? My husband was not a man to show love, to show his emotions very well. And Joshua was a lot like him, always a little distant, not one to show his true feelings, I mean."

She stopped abruptly and sat for a minute with her eyes downcast. Dylan couldn't tell if she were embarrassed for talking so much about her family or if she were merely gathering her thoughts together. Finally, Mrs. Petersen began again. "Josh was in high school when the accident happened, and he left here as soon as he graduated later that year."

"So you were completely on your own, then?" Dylan inquired.

"Yes. And it's been hard. There was an insurance policy, but the company refused to pay off since it didn't happen at work. I remember Josh was upset, very upset. He felt we had been gypped of money that was rightfully ours. Josh said common, ordinary folk like us were always being taken advantage of. He often said that he would get even with them, would get a lot of money of his own, but, of course, he was just a young boy; there was nothing he could do."

"Where did your husband work, Mrs. Petersen?" Dylan held up his mug for a refill, and the woman hurried to get the coffee pot. She poured the hot drink into his cup, being careful not to let any drip onto the table's yellow Formica top.

"He had worked for years at Lyndale Steel—just as a foreman. Nate—that's his nickname; his name was Nathaniel, but most people called him Nate—never seemed to want to move up in the company. Josh hated this. He worked at Lyndale's during summers while in high school."

"So Joshua considered staying at Lyndale Steel?"

"Definitely not, Mr. Dylan. That's what he and his father argued about. Joshua was very smart in school, a real good student in math, and he was good with his hands also, but his dad never gave him credit for having a brain. Josh wanted to go on to college, but his dad kept insisting that there was no money. I remember Josh saying that was always the excuse for everything—no money. Having money was always very, very important to my son."

"So you don't know if Joshua ever went on to college?"

"No. I imagine he did, if he had the chance. He always told me that he would be rich some day. But you know how that is; it's just any boy's dream."

"Well, Mrs. Petersen, if I do find out anything at all, I'll make sure the information is sent on to you. But, so far I haven't really been able to find out why Joshua has disappeared. I certainly hope—feel actually—that nothing bad has happened to him. Sometimes people simply seem to vanish without any plausible explanation." Dylan got up to leave.

"Well, I do get a nice money order every year around Christmas but no letter," the woman added. "I'm sure the money is from Josh, and it's a big help in paying the taxes on this house."

"Can you tell me where the money is mailed from?"

"Oh, the envelopes come from all over the country, and I guess since Josh hasn't seen fit to let me know where he's been all these years, I guess I shouldn't worry. Still he is my baby, and I would like to believe that he is well and happy somewhere." She smiled shyly. "You know how it is. A mother always hopes for the best when it comes to her child."

Dylan thanked Karen Petersen again and drove back toward the hotel. What a sad situation, he thought. That old woman, alone, wondering, worrying. Still, with the way things were shaping up, she might be better off not knowing where Joshua was and what he was up to next.

After a light lunch of bass, corn muffins and fresh corn, Dylan strolled through Duluth's Maritime Museum, stopping briefly to study the information on the sinking of the freighter, Edmund Fitzgerald. He needed some distraction to try and get his thoughts together. There was something nagging him about Joshua Petersen; a little voice in his head kept saying, "Something's wrong with all of this. Things just don't add up."

Leaving the museum he decided to visit the high school which Petersen had attended. He arrived there just as the marching band was starting its practice and stopped for a moment to listen to a squeaky version of Sousa. Fortunately, the school principal, Hal Anderson, was in his office and willing to talk. Dylan could tell by the casual dress of Anderson that he wasn't expecting any visitors.

"Yes, I do remember Joshua Petersen. I'm sorry to say there are many students whom I can't recall, but Petersen was something special. He was always on the honor roll; very, very bright in the math area; won a math competition that one of our local banks sponsored. That was a feather in the school's cap."

"He was a well-rounded student, then?" Dylan asked.

"Well, noooo. He worked after school for a garage, I believe. So that didn't leave him much free time. Joshua did take several of the shop classes—auto mechanics, wood shop—the usual."

"I spoke briefly with Mrs. Petersen this morning," Dylan broke in. "She mentioned that Joshua's father was dead."

"Yeah. That was a great tragedy. Happened in the winter of Joshua's senior year. Mr. Peterson was hit by a train."

"Really," Dylan nodded his head in understanding. "An accident?"

"Yes. It was decidedly an accident, brakes gave out unexpectedly on his car. I was afraid the accident would affect Joshua's school work, but he seemed to handle it much better than anyone would have expected. Of course, he was a resilient kid."

"I'm not sure I understand what you mean by 'resilient," Dylan asked.

"Well, I guess I'm trying to say that Joshua pretty much accepted what was dealt out to him. He didn't show a great deal of grief, at least where anyone could see it. That's what I meant."

Dylan studied the notes he had been making in his small notebook. "I guess that's all of the questions I have. I do appreciate your help, Mr. Anderson." Dylan moved closer to the door but hesitated. "I don't suppose any of his former teachers would be around today, would they?"

"No, summer vacation most people stay clear of this

place if they can. However, Burt Donner, his auto mechanics instructor, runs a gas station and garage during the summer and off hours. If you want, I could call and see if he would talk with you."

"I would like that very much," Dylan said as Anderson began to dial the phone.

A few minutes of telephone conversation and Dylan was on his way to Burt's Garage.

Burt Donner was a huge man with a leathery skin and thick black hair. His face was streaked with grease, and he wiped his hands on a filthy towel as he moved out from under the hood of a 1965 Plymouth.

"You must be the detective?" Donner started to shake hands and then drew his back. "Guess I'd better not or you'll be dirty like me."

"Looks like you have a pretty nice little business here," Dylan said, looking around the shop.

"Can't complain. Keeps me awfully busy though what with my teaching during the winter months."

"Mr. Anderson indicated to me that you might remember one of your former students, Joshua Petersen?" Dylan asked the question, but he had the suspicion that as soon as he had left Anderson's office, the principal had called Donner back and explained fully the reason why Dylan was in town.

"Sure, remember him well. Had him in beginning, intermediate and advanced auto mechanics. Tall, good looking young fellow. That kid had a good head on his shoulders. He was a real whiz at figuring things out. By the time I got through with him, he could have built a car from scratch."

"He liked to do that kind of work, did he?"

"Well, I don't know that exactly. But he was good at what he did. He told me his dad wanted him to be good with his hands."

What Dylan was hearing was repetitive. He thanked Donner for his help and drove slowly back to his motel. It was nearing four o'clock, and several shop owners were cranking down green and white striped awnings against the late afternoon sun. He thought a dip in the pool sounded good.

Around eight forty-five the next morning Dylan arrived at Lyndale Steel. For a few minutes after he got out of his car, he watched a freighter loaded with iron ore edging into the dock. Lake Superior shone a deep crystal blue in the morning sun. Dylan thought, "It's summer here, but that sure looks cold."

Making his way to the manager's office, Dylan patiently explained to an aging clerk whose gray hair straggled in wisps from the pile atop her head why he was there. "If possible, I'd like to see someone who would remember Nate Petersen or his son Joshua."

"Why I remember both of them," the woman volunteered as she stuck a pencil into her hair, further loosening the already untidy bun. "Well, actually I remember Nate because he worked here for so many years. I used to be in payroll and saw him once a week when he picked up his paycheck."

"You don't remember his son?"

"I remember seeing him a few times, but I think he was only a part-time worker." The woman thought for a minute. "But you know, I'm sure John Small could help you since he worked with Nate. He's a foreman now. Let me see if he's working today."

As he waited for the woman to locate Small, Dylan looked around the office. It was cramped and littered with papers piled on two battered desks pushed into one corner. Faded wood paneling was on three walls, and the rust-colored carpet was worn and water stained in several spots from a leaky roof. Greasy smudges left by laborers accented the entryway. Ash trays were overflowing with lipstick-smeared cigarette butts and chewing gum wrappers. On the wall over one desk a calendar with a photo of Diamond Head was the only bright spot in the office. Delightful place to spend one's life, Dylan thought.

"Small says to come right down; he's got a few minutes to talk with you. Just go down the stairs on your right and then follow that long corridor." The clerk pointed over Dylan's head.

John Small shook hands with Dylan and motioned him to a cubbyhole in one corner of the large foundry. He was a huge man with a thick neck set on massive shoulders. It looks like he could load sixteen tons. Dylan could almost hear the words from the old popular song.

"It's quieter in here, Mr. Dylan," Small said, as he shut the door behind them, somewhat dimming the noise of the pistons.

To Dylan it still sounded like the boiler room on a destroyer—incessant banging that made one's ears ring.

"Sarah said you had some questions for me?"

"I was wondering if you remember Nate Petersen and his son?" Dylan had not learned that the clerk's name was

Sarah. He would make a point to stop by and thank her for her help and call her by name.

"Yes, I remember Nate well. We worked side by side for over twenty years. Were good friends."

"His son?" Dylan prodded. "He worked here at Lyndale also."

"Yeah, a couple of summers. The kid didn't like it though, didn't want to be just a mill hand."

"Was he a good worker?"

"He was all right. Always on time. Had a good head on him. Really a bright kid. Probably this wasn't the place for him."

"Still, he didn't look for other work?"

"Not that I recall," Small hesitated. "I remember his dad was really upset with him most of the time. Said the kid had big notions. Too big for his britches was the way Nate put it. Said the kid thought he was better than his dad. Then, too, I think the kid was sort of sweet on one of the local gals. Maybe that's why he kept working here. Needed the money for his sparking."

Sparking. Dylan couldn't remember actually hearing someone refer to dating as "sparking." But this was something new. Karen Petersen had emphatically said that Joshua had no interest in dating. "Did he go with any one girl in particular?" Dylan inquired.

"Well," Small hesitated, "that's been a while ago. I do remember seeing him and Ella Porter together quite a bit. Ella Lansdorf her name was then. She's been married long time now, got married right out of high school. Course, there could have been others. I didn't keep up with the young crowd."

Changing the subject, Dylan said. "I talked with Mrs. Petersen. She said her husband was killed in an accident."

"Jesus! It was some accident. Worst thing I'd ever seen. Car parts stretched for what seemed like miles. I still think about it sometimes. This town hasn't seen anything that bad since then." Small shook his head.

"A train accident Mrs. Petersen said."

"Yeah. It was a Friday night. Nate and I had stopped off for a beer at Two Moose Crossing. We shot a game of pool, had another beer and then decided to call it a night. It wasn't late—dark, of course—but only about 8:00 P.M. He had left just before me and was going down the hill toward home. I was right behind him since we only lived a few blocks apart. The night freight was passing through town, and he just seemed to shoot right under one of the boxcars. His Chevy burst into flames and was dragged about 200 yards. It was cut into pieces from the weight of the fully loaded boxcars. The engineer couldn't stop the train for a long ways." Small ceased speaking again and stared into space.

"So he drove under the train? He didn't try to stop?" Dylan asked.

"Oh, he tried to stop. His brake lights came on, but the car didn't seem to slow down one little bit. There was wreckage strewn all along the rails. Parts of Nate's body hung from the burnt out wreckage of the auto. It was God awful. Never seen anything like it before, not even the accidents that happen here at the mill."

"You said the brakes didn't work?"

"Hell, I don't know. Didn't look like it to me."

"Do you know if the police checked this out?" Dylan

wanted to see if Small had given any information to the police at the scene.

"Yeah, but these guys here wouldn't know a train wreck from a plane wreck. We don't have any of those big shot city detectives up here. It was just listed as an accident, although the possibility of suicide was mentioned."

"Suicide?" Dylan asked in surprise. "Do you think Nate Petersen committed suicide?"

"Hell no! I just had a beer with him. He was in a good mood. I would of known if he was gonna commit suicide. We were friends."

"And his son," Dylan inquired. "How did Joshua take his dad's death?"

"Oh, hell. Who knows about things like that. Josh was a funny kid. Didn't say much. Didn't show much. Nate's wife took it pretty hard, but the kid ... he just seemed to go on as usual. Left town not too long afterwards. Went into the service I heard, soon as he graduated high school."

"Well, you've been very helpful, and I appreciate you taking time to talk with me," Dylan said, again shaking Small's hand. On his way out to the car, Dylan remembered to also stop in and thank Sarah. He thought of trying to track down Ella Lansdorf Porter but finally decided that she probably could add little to what he already knew.

Dylan drove back to Minneapolis and booked a flight for California early the next morning. He was now certain that Peterson/Robinson/Proteus was not simply a thief; he was also a murderer. "Much more dangerous than anyone knew," Dylan thought. "I'll bet if the truth were known, he rigged the brakes on his dad's car and on his convertible that killed his Air Force buddy." Dylan shook his head, muttering to himself. "Two murders and no one became suspicious. It seems he's gotten away free."

Later that night he called his wife. "I'll be arriving home on the 11:20 a.m. flight. Honey, you wouldn't believe this. I'm not sure I can do anything of value for Vickers. This guy just doesn't exist. He's one person to some people and a completely different person to others. Literally. As near as I can tell he's had at least two different identities, and I think he must have come up with another one in Houston. I'm going to see if there are some records on his blood type. He can change his identity, but he can't change his blood type."

Barbara Dylan waited patiently. She knew her husband often used her as a sounding board and didn't expect a response. When he finally stopped speaking, she asked, "Are you going to be home for a while?"

"Yeah, I guess so. I don't really know what else I can do right now, and I need to report to Cybertech. They may wonder how I'm spending their money." Dylan laughed.

"I'll be at the airport to meet you. Maybe we can stop for lunch."

"That's great. I can run more of my trip info by you. Maybe you will see something I'm overlooking."

"I doubt that," Barbara replied. She knew Dylan was very thorough in any research he did, whether it was for the books he authored or if he were working on occasional cases.

"You know, there is one thing you could do," Dylan shot back.

"Name it. I've got a few hours to kill after the kids are off to school."

"I remember that Bill Robinson smoked a particular brand of tobacco. Could you put in a couple of calls around L.A. and see if you can get me the addresses of some tobacco shops in the Anaheim area or around Santa Monica?"

"I'll try. See you soon." Barbara Dylan hung up the phone and sighed deeply. She had been married to Charles Dylan long enough to know a great deal about him. There was nothing he loved better than a good puzzle, and it looked like he had found one in the Bill Robinson case. Once he took on an assignment, whether from the police or in the private sector, he pursued it doggedly until he brought it to a satisfactory close. Their life would not run smoothly until her husband had solved this missing persons case.

Todd had a problem, a big problem and one that was going to require some action. The problem was one Tina Zabinski! He could tolerate her gushing invitations; he could tolerate her blatant sexuality; what he couldn't tolerate was her incessant snooping.

He had wanted to stay secluded, but Tina wouldn't allow that. She was the epitome of the good neighbor, wanting to make everyone she knew feel welcome. He had gone along with her, just as he had played the part at Cybertech. He had been friendly to a certain extent, enough so that she wouldn't wonder about him or bother him more than she did. Several times he had agreed to a dinner date or an early drive into the hills. He had even considered inviting her into his bed, as she had hinted on more than one occasion that she would not turn down such an invitation. However, he had decided that the cost for his sexual gratification would be much too high.

Unlike her roommate Rhonda, Tina had to be the nosiest individual he had ever met. She constantly was grilling him about his writing, about his past, about his future plans—everything. What was worse she wouldn't keep her mouth shut. Twice he had nearly been caught in one of his fabrications when Rhonda had mentioned something that he had told Tina. Tina seemed to think that what he did was exciting, and she blabbed to anyone whether they listened or not.

A couple of weeks ago he had found her at his desk, idly looking over his mail. She had apologized, and he had made light of it, saying something like, "We might as well be married if you're going to check my bank statements."

Then just last week he had come home from an overnight junket and found Tina waiting for him in his house.

"What's going on," he finally managed, looking around the room to see if there had been a robbery or vandalism. He had casually asked Tina to keep an eye on the place while he was gone.

"I just thought I'd come over and have dinner almost ready when you got back. Sort of a surprise."

It was a big surprise. He hardly knew what to say. "How'd you get in?" Todd finally asked.

"Well, I showed the place a couple of times for the rental agent—you know, Mr. Gomez—and I just sort of kept a key."

Great, Todd thought. Gomez had not mentioned that there were extra keys to the place. How could Todd have anticipated that problem? You didn't rent a place and expect to have to change all of the locks on the doors to insure privacy.

"I didn't really expect dinner, Tina," he began. What should he say? What did she expect?

"It was no trouble. Just a casserole and salad."

"Well, I guess we should eat then," he said, trying to keep the exasperation out of his voice. "Thanks." He was livid at this invasion of his privacy but thought it best not to show it.

The casserole was some strange concoction of shell fish but very tasty, and the salad was crisp and appetizing. They shared a bottle of Chardonnay, and he was just beginning to relax a little when Tina abruptly asked, "You're not really Todd Walker, are you?"

For a moment he was dumbfounded. "What are you talking about?"

"I was doing some straightening up—you're not the neatest person in the world, are you—and I went to hang some clothes in your closet. What's with the black wig I saw on the shelf?"

Slowly he reached for his glass of wine and took a sip. He waited for a few minutes, trying to think what to do. How could this dumb broad stumble into his life and upset his plans to such an extent? Finally, he took one of Tina's hands in his and smiled ruefully. "You're absolutely right. I'm not Todd Walker."

"I knew it! I knew it! I just knew from the first time I met you that you were hiding something. Come on, tell. You're a bank robber. That's how you can afford to live like this."

He waited another moment and then said teasingly, "You live pretty well yourself, and I didn't think you were a bank robber."

"Oh, you know what I mean. But tell me. Who are you really?"

By now he had gotten his thoughts together. "Okay. My name is really Anthony Stevens. I've been using Todd

Walker because I'm going through a very messy divorce—
very, very messy. My wife, actually she should be my
ex-wife by now, has been trying to locate me to see if she
can collect some more money from me. I'm really a writer.
That is the truth, and I do have a publisher. So, as you
can see, I don't want her to know about this book or the
advance and royalties that may come due from it. Can you
understand that?"

"Of course I can," Tina responded, applying pressure to
his hand. "Why didn't you tell me this before? I know how
it is to have money problems. Where is your wife now?"

"Beats me," he replied. "I imagine she's still in the Boston
area. Remember, I told you originally I was from Boston."

"Well, at least most of what you've told me is true,"
Tina pouted coyly.

"Tina," he said, his tone becoming more serious, "I want
you to do me a big favor. Please, please don't tell anyone
else about this. I don't need questions from everyone we
know on this beach. Also, in case my wife might be able to
track me to this area, I want everyone to continue thinking
I'm Todd Walker."

"You can trust me," Tina emphasized the word trust.
"Now, finish your dinner. I won't tell a soul."

She would try to keep her promise, he knew. However,
eventually she would not be able to resist and the story he
had given her would be all over the beach. Something had
to be done; he could not let Tina Zabinski alter his plans.
His agenda called for him to stay in Santa Monica until
mid-October.

Dylan was home only briefly and then took off the next day to check on the various tobacco stores which Barbara had located for him. He checked three in Anaheim with no luck. On Wilshire, close to A. A. Cybertech, Dylan tried again at a store in a nearby mall.

"I'm looking for a guy who might be one of your customers and who smokes this kind of tobacco." Dylan handed the man a small white envelope containing the sample he had picked up at Robinson's home.

"Not too many people request that blend," the clerk replied after sniffing the contents of the envelope. "Who wants to know?"

Dylan explained that the customer he was trying to locate had disappeared while on a business trip, and the company he worked for was very concerned that he had met with an accident. Dylan was merely trying to find information that would lead to the missing man. The explanation seemed to satisfy the clerk.

"What's the guy look like?"

Dylan showed him a photo which had been reprinted

from the wedding photograph as it was too awkward to carry around.

"Seems like I do recall him. He came in fairly frequently; well, about once a month. Didn't say too much but always asked for Schermerhorn. That's what's you gave me. He's been coming here for....gee, five years or more."

"Have you seen him lately?"

"No, now that you mention it; he hasn't been in for a couple of months."

"Do you recognize him as Bill Robinson?"

"He never said what his last name was, and I never asked. But I do know his first name was Bill. We would chat briefly, so we used first names now and then."

"Has anyone else asked for this particular blend lately?"

"Yes, there are a couple of other men who use it, but none of them fit this photo. Both are quite a bit older."

Another lead gone, Dylan thought. That was about his last one. Where was he going to go from here? He thanked the clerk and started out the shop door.

"Oh, sorry," Dylan apologized as he bumped into a tall, blonde man with a camera case slung over his shoulder.

"Hi," Todd greeted the clerk in the tobacco shop. "Got any Schermerhorn?

"Funny you should ask," the clerk said as he began to rummage among cans of tobacco in a cabinet behind the counter. He produced a bulky can with white wrapping. "The guy that just passed you was asking about this same stuff."

"Oh!" Todd turned to see the back of a large man ambling slowly down the mall. "Does he smoke my brand?"

"Nope. He was looking for some business man who has disappeared. Name is Bill something. I don't think he mentioned the last name."

"Did he say why the man had disappeared?" Todd leaned companionably on the counter. "I'm a writer; might be an interesting story here."

"No. Just said it was under mysterious circumstances. I'll bet the guy murdered his wife or something like that."

"So you couldn't help him?"

"I tried. I looked at the photo he showed me, and I recognized the guy. I never forget a face, especially a customer who has been coming in for years. But I haven't seen the guy for a couple of months now."

Todd paid for the tobacco and hurried out into the mall. Obviously the shopkeeper forgot my face, Todd thought. He was pleased that his disguise had held up so well. He scanned the backs of shoppers, hoping to catch another glimpse of the "investigator." About half way down the mall he spotted the man, standing at the counter of a coffee vendor. The man carried his styrofoam cup to a small table situated near a waterfall surrounded by potted greenery.

Todd hung back for a few minutes and then also purchased a coffee. Casually he took a table across from the man, removed his camera from its case and proceeded to busy himself loading film. When this was accomplished, he stood up and began to take a series of photos. Getting down on one knee, he aimed the camera at the shops on the mall's second level. Then he took several shots of the shoppers as they made their way up and down the escalators and spilled out into the shops. Finally Todd turned his camera on the waterfall, being careful to include the investigator in one of the photos. Then he sat back down and drank his coffee.

Dylan had idly watched the man scanning the mall with his camera. Photographer for an advertising agency, he concluded. Might be an interesting job. He drained the last bit of coffee from the cup, tossing it into a trash bin as he made his way toward the mall exit. That tobacco shop had been a dead end, but he still had two others to check out.

About thirty feet back, Todd Walker followed Dylan

into the mall parking lot. Again, Todd was pleased with his disguise. Although he now knew that he was being pursued and that a picture of him as Bill Robinson was being shown to various people, the investigator had not recognized him as Todd Walker. Now, what he badly needed to know was the identity of his pursuer. He wasn't a cop or the tobacco shop owner would have mentioned this. So who was he? A private investigator? An insurance investigator?

As Dylan drove away, Todd wrote down the license plate number on Dylan's car. By tonight he would know the man's identity as he would call the DMV. Todd started his convertible and drove out of the parking lot, keeping far enough back so that he could follow inconspicuously. After nearly an hour, he ended up watching the man get out of his car in a faculty parking lot at Pepperdine University and enter a building marked School of Social Sciences.

Todd waited for over an hour before he finally decided to get something to eat. Why would a university professor be asking questions about Bill Robinson? He'd go over it in his mind bit by bit and see if there were anything that would help him know how the hunt for Bill Robinson was going. On the way to the restaurant, however, he needed to stop at a hardware store and pick up some super glue. He also needed some rubber gloves and duct tape.

Todd's late lunch was leisurely. He started with some sushi and then had a small porterhouse. The restaurant was located across the street from the beach, and he idly watched the pale tourists getting their annual doses of sunburn. A seagull meandered along the sand, its wings tucked in back like a little old man out for an afternoon stroll.

"So, someone is still looking for Bill Robinson." Thoughts raced through Todd's mind. "What a fluke. I actually bumped into the guy. But who is he? Surely the police have moved on to other things by now. I'm glad I was able to get a photo of him and discover where he works. What luck! Who would have thought such a chance meeting would occur."

Todd ordered a slice of chocolate cheese cake and a refill of tea. "The man knew about the special tobacco, so that meant he had either talked with someone at Cybertech or Margaret put him on to it. Well, better not go to the tobacco shop again just in case this guy might return. In fact, better change his brand of tobacco."

Todd settled his check, left the waitress a couple of two dollar bills as a tip and drove back to the beach house. He had been on the beach nearly five months but planned on staying six months to let the trail get cold. Soon, he hoped, everyone would run out of leads. Certainly the tobacco store clerk would have been of no help.

He saw Tina coming up the beach, the straps on her white bikini trailing down over her shoulders. "That woman must have extra sensory perception," he said aloud. "She always seems to know when I'm home.

As Tina waved to him, Todd figured that he would have about an hour before she would appear at his door, two cold drinks in hand, and urge him out onto the deck for an hour of chatter before she had to leave for work. That gave him enough time to locate the investigator's license plate.

Charles Dylan, Agoura Hills, the DMV clerk said in

a bored voice. A big smile creased Todd's face. He would have to go and visit this Charles Dylan, without Dylan knowing it, of course. Might see his family, if he had one. Look around at the university.

"So, Mr. Charles Dylan," Todd grumbled to himself, "who are you and why are you the one to be tracking me? I'm going to have to find out more about you. Maybe you'll have to meet with an accident."

"Well, it looks like you've been paying for nothing," Dylan began as he settled into the leather chair at A. A. Cybertech and accepted the usual cup of coffee from Vicker's secretary. "So far, I haven't found your man, and I'm at a dead end."

"What do you mean nothing?" Vickers shot back. "Nothing in over eight weeks?"

"Oh, I've found out a lot, but nothing that is of any help to us. Or to the police, if you decide to let them know about the theft." Dylan decided to add a small amount of cream to his coffee and then carefully placed the china creamer back on the silver tray.

Taking a quick sip of the hot brew, Dylan looked first at Vickers and then at Nolan, who had just hurried into the office. "First, Bill Robinson died in 1973 in Vietnam."

"Died?" Vickers leaned forward in his chair. "How could he have died if he worked here? Are you certain you have the right Robinson?"

"Definitely. It's quite apparent that your employee

was in the military—just as Margaret Robinson indicated and as he told you. However, who he was is another question. He definitely was not Bill Robinson, then or now."

"So he was using a false name," Nolan asked.

"Yes. As far as I can surmise, he must have had access to military computer records, just as he did here. His real name is Joshua Nathaniel Petersen. Born and reared in Minnesota. When he left the Air Force, he merely took another name. I requested that the Air Force Office of Special Investigation do some checking on him, and they got this information back to me. Quickly I might add." Dylan took another sip of coffee and placed the cup on the small table next to where he was sitting.

"How about his wife? Could she be involved in this?" Vickers interrupted.

"I thought of that, but it's very unlikely. I talked with her at length. She seems to know less about her husband than I do—which is very little."

"But she was married to him—how long?" Nolan looked at Dylan.

"A little over three years, according to the marriage certificate, and that's what his wife confirmed. I saw the wedding photo—your typical bride and groom shot—displayed in their home. But there was nothing to indicate he had ever been in the military, except what she told me, and that was almost nothing. She said he didn't like to talk about his military experience."

"I can understand why," Nolan interjected sarcastically.

"American Airlines supplied the local police with

their passenger manifest from the flight Robinson was supposed to be on," Dylan continued. "Took me forever but I eventually was able to contact each person listed. There was one I couldn't locate."

"The flight into L.A. If he were taking money from us and living here, why would he come back home?" Vickers looked puzzled. "That doesn't make sense."

"If he's as shrewd as he appears to be, this is the place he'd come. This would be the last place you'd look for him, right?"

"You've made your point," Vickers replied. "We never even considered L.A. Every other place in America but never L.A. But how would you find him here?"

"That is the point," Dylan got up and went to the window. "You won't find him." He gestured toward the outside. "Look out there. Millions of people—at least ten million people in Southern California alone. He's just one of them. He could be anywhere."

"So where does this leave us?" Nolan asked.

"As I said at the beginning—nowhere. I asked Margaret Robinson if he had any quirks, anything he spent a lot of time doing, a hobby—anything. He didn't! I've talked with his co-workers at length here at Cybertec. Nothing! They all thought he was a great guy."

Dylan sat back down and reached for his coffee. By now it was only lukewarm. Nolan offered to get him a fresh cup but Dylan declined. He needed to finish his report.

"As far as I can ascertain the only things that might even be considered different about Robinson are that he smokes a pretty rare and expensive tobacco, and he apparently would frequently give a two-dollar bill to the children of his friends and would occasionally leave a two-dollar bill as a tip for a waitress. They thought this was unusual because he would have had to get the money, generally, at a bank. There aren't too many two-dollar bills just running around in normal circulation." Dylan paused.

"Is that really an important point?" Nolan interjected.

"Could be... or not. We know someone who seems to fit Robinson's description was in the Prop Wash, a Houston airport bar. The waitress felt she recognized the photo I was showing around, and she volunteered that she remembered the man because he tipped with a two-dollar bill. Of course, it could be coincidence, but Robinson was supposed to be in that airport. Then, too, if he's in the habit of using these bills, for some reason or other, he might not change that habit. It's a little thing like that which cause people to be caught. On the other hand, he may never use a two-dollar bill again."

"I guess I don't fully realize why he did this," Nolan said. "Why did he steal the money? Was he in debt? Did he gamble and owe money?"

"No, I don't think that's it at all," Dylan replied. "From what I can tell talking with his mother and other people who knew him as a young man, he's doing this strictly for the money—for himself. I think his agenda is such that he merely wants to get a great deal of money; his family was fairly poor, and he simply wants to be wealthy. He's going to be awfully hard to trace."

"So, there's no hope of catching him, of getting any of the money back, of even finding the bastard?" Vickers said in a resigned voice. "That's it?"

"Unless something else turns up," Dylan agreed. "However, on the airlines passenger manifest I mentioned earlier, there was the name Mark Proteus. I can't locate any such person. I think your former employee is one cocky son-of-a-bitch. I think he is showing all of us how clever he is. I'm certain that Mark Proteus is Bill Robinson. So I've given Robinson, whoever he really is, the name he selected—Proteus."

"Proteus?" Nolan looked confused.

"Yes," Dylan replied. "Like the Greek God Proteus, our man seems to be able to change his identity whenever he needs to and just vanish."

"Tomorrow's gonna be a scorcher, unusual for September," the weather man grinned out of the TV screen. As soon as the newscast was over, Todd made preparations to put his plan into action.

He thought the two women next door would never go to bed, but finally around two-thirty, the lights went out. He waited another hour and then crept into the neighboring carport. Cautiously, he opened the door of Tina's Datsun and slapped a piece of duct tape over the interior light switch. Working as quickly as possible, he switched the heating and air conditioning controls so that they would work in reverse. He was thankful now for the hours spent in auto shop as the knowledge he had gained there had come in handy several times.

Unscrewing both vents in the dash, Todd placed two small bottles of super glue inside, removed their caps and, checking carefully to be sure the inner seal had been pierced, replaced the vent screens. He was satisfied that once Tina turned on the air conditioning, the fumes from the super glue would fill the car and as she drove away from home would shortly asphyxiate her. Stripping the duct tape off, he checked the dashboard; everything appeared normal. Quietly, he shut the car door and returned home. Now, if the weather would cooperate.

As the weather man had predicted the night before, it had the makings of a scorcher. Perfect, Todd thought as he tossed a few things into a bag. Just what I needed.

Around ten o'clock Tina appeared on her deck as she usually did, a mug of coffee in one hand and a cigarette in the other. Todd waited a few minutes and then casually strolled outside himself.

"Going to be a hot one today," he said in greeting.

"Oh, how true," Tina smiled, still not fully awake.

"Thought I ought to tell you, and you might mention it also to Rhonda, I'm going to be away for a few days. Have to do some research in the Big Bear area."

"Lucky you. I wish I could go along. Maybe it would be cooler up there, and it's such pretty country."

"Well, keep an eye on my place again, won't you."

"Sure, darling. Everything will be just the same when you return."

A few hours later Todd cruised slowly to a stop in front of the Dylan home in Agoura Hills. He could see the open hood of a 1975 Ford and the rear end and shapely legs of a woman with the rest of her body hidden from view.

"Can I help?" he asked softly.

"Oh," Barbara Dylan exclaimed in a startled voice as she jerked her head from under the hood. "I didn't hear you come up."

"I'm sorry. I didn't mean to startle you." Todd smiled apologetically.

"It's all right. I just can't get this damn car started." Barbara pushed a stray lock of hair out of one eye and carefully appraised Todd. "Do I know you?"

"I'm sorry," Todd said again. "I'm looking for Charles Dylan. I thought he lived here. I'm an old friend of his—Todd Walker's the name." He grinned. "I'm just here for a few hours and thought I'd take a chance on finding him at home. Is this the right place?"

"It certainly is, Mr. Walker, but Charles is at the university. He has classes on Tuesday and Thursday."

"Well, I'm sorry I can't take the time to try and find him there. I only have about a half hour before I have to be on my way to Frisco. Have a late afternoon appointment there."

"He'll be so sorry to have missed you. Can't I offer you a cup of coffee or a cold drink, Mr. Walker?"

"Call me Todd, and, yes, I would take a cup of coffee if you have it already made."

Dylan had only been home a few minutes when he heard his wife's car drive up. Both children raced into the house with just a brief "hello" for their dad and then disappeared upstairs.

"What a day," Barbara began as she walked in, carrying several boxes in her arms. "I picked up some rolls and a pie at the bakery. I'll get dinner started right now, but the kids are going to spend the night at the Collins'. Some pajama party. It will be just the two of us." She headed for the kitchen.

"Why don't we just grab something out," Dylan suggested. "My day has been hectic, too."

"Great idea. I'm glad you took my hint." Barbara came back into the den and flopped down in an easy chair. "I'll change to something a little less messy in a few minutes."

"You do look a little windblown," Dylan smiled at her. "What was so bad about your day?"

"Oh, that damn car wouldn't start. You've got to get that starter fixed or get me another car. If it hadn't been for that old friend of yours, I'd never have gotten everything done. I thought I was going to have to call a tow."

"Old friend of mine," Dylan looked puzzled. "What old friend is that?"

"The one from the Marines. The one you were at camp with. You know, Todd Walker."

"Todd Walker," he repeated automatically. He couldn't remember ever knowing anyone named Todd Walker.

"Yes, he was very nice. I wanted him to stay longer, but he said he had to be in San Francisco later today. He said he had seen you at a distance the other day in a mall in L.A. but couldn't catch up with you. Helped me get my car going after we had coffee."

"He came in?" Dylan tried to make his voice conversational, but he could feel the hair rise on the back of his neck.

"Yes, of course. What would you think of me if I didn't ask a friend in?" Barbara replied indignantly.

Dylan yawned and stretched, taking time to cover his surprise and anxiety. "Well, I'm sorry I missed him. Maybe he'll stop by on his way back."

"Maybe," Barbara replied. "He didn't say." She changed the subject as she walked out of the room. "I'm going up to dress now. If I have time, I'd like to take a shower. I really feel grubby."

Dylan didn't respond. He was remembering a conversation with one of his graduate assistants earlier in the day. What was it the young man had said? "Professor Dylan, I've got an extra paper here from the exam you had me give yesterday. A name I don't see on our class records. Bill Roberts or Robinson. It's hard to make out the handwriting, and it's not a very good exam."

At the time the name had brought a very uneasy feeling, but he had told himself that it was simply a coincidence, that it was just some student filling out an extra exam as a joke or someone who had been late in registering for the course. Bill Robinson was not an unusual name. The Bill Robinson he had been chasing didn't know him, couldn't have known that he had been hired by Cybertech. Suddenly, he knew he was wrong. Robinson must have been in the shopping mall near the tobacco store and seen him leaving the place. Still, how could Robinson have known who he was? Dylan suddenly had a queasy feeling in the pit of his stomach.

Walker must be the name Robinson was using now, and he had been right here, at his home, in his house, having coffee with his wife. The thoughts tumbled out of his mind. Proteus, the man he had named Proteus, was now going around as Todd Walker and had somehow tracked Dylan down. He had gone to Pepperdine, put the name Bill Robinson on a test, taunting Dylan, to let him know he was aware of being hunted. Suddenly Dylan laughed loudly, "The tracked tracks the tracker."

However, it was not a laughing matter. This man could be dangerous, he knew. He was fairly certain that Proteus had already used his knowledge of automobile engines to kill two people. And he had helped fix Barbara's car. Fix it?

"Oh, my God," he said aloud."

"Oh, my God, what?" Barbara asked from the doorway. She had put on a sleeveless black dress with a gold chain and brushed her hair. "What's wrong?"

"Nothing you have to worry about," Dylan covered

quickly. "Just something I forgot to do at the school. I'll have to call first thing tomorrow and see that it's done. No big problem." He ushered Barbara out to the car.

Over dinner, Dylan was preoccupied. Finally, Barbara asked, "What's bothering you? You've hardly said a word. Is something wrong with your food? Wine not good?"

"Sorry," Dylan apologized. "I guess I was just mulling over the visit by Walker. I've wracked my mind and can't recall anyone with a name even close to Todd Walker."

"Now that I think about it, we didn't get into many details about your friendship with him. Mainly he was interested in what you were doing—what the family was doing."

"Great," Dylan thought. "Now Walker has even more information on me." However, he didn't want to arouse Barbara's curiosity by continuing the conversation on his old acquaintance. Pouring a little white wine into her glass, he casually said, "Oh, well, no big issue, but in the future you might want to think twice about inviting strange men into the house."

Dylan slept badly and was up early the next morning. He had already had juice and coffee when Barbara came down.

"Where are you off to so early? It's just a few minutes after eight." She took a coffee mug from the cupboard and poured herself a steaming cup, adding a dollop of cream and some sugar. "Want me to fix some bacon and eggs?"

"No, thanks but I've got to take that car of yours into the shop. Can't have strange men taking care of my wife. I don't have an appointment, but if I get there early, they may get it fixed today," Dylan replied, giving her a quick kiss before going out the door.

While the car was being worked on at the garage, Dylan took the time to again go over the visit by Proteus-Walker. Carefully he re-examined all the points which had kept him awake during the night. First, Proteus knew who he was, knew where he lived and, now, knew quite a bit about his family. He had discovered the latter during last evening's dinner as Barbara casually chatted about her conversation with his old friend Todd Walker. Although

Proteus apparently had seen him near the mall tobacco shop, how he had discovered Dylan's name and located him was the big mystery. Was Proteus still in contact with someone at Cybertech? That didn't seem reasonable. Still, he had no way of knowing what was reasonable.

Second, Proteus had been at the university, had been confident enough to sit in on Dylan's lectures. It was a big class of over two hundred students; he hardly knew any of them by name unless they had stopped by his office to discuss material for a research paper or to check on a grade. Besides, would he have recognized Proteus from the original photo he had of Bill Robinson? Barbara had described the man as blonde and suntanned. Obviously, Proteus had a totally new appearance.

Third, where was Proteus now? Was he still in the area, lurking near the house or sitting in the cafeteria waiting for Dylan's next lecture? He had a fleeting sense of panic. Should he cancel classes, send Barbara and the kids away. No. He would have to give Barbara a reason, and he didn't want her or the children to be worried.

"Calm down," he murmured. "Relax. Take it easy." He wasn't thinking logically. If Proteus had wanted to harm him or Barbara, he would already have done so—could easily have done so. Proteus wanted Dylan to be scared, scared so that he would stop his tracking. So, Proteus didn't have a contact at Cybertech or he would already have known that Dylan was off the case. "Have been off the case," Dylan said aloud. "But I guess that maybe since he's located me, I'll need to be looking for him from now on." He grinned self-consciously as another man waiting in the garage gave him an odd look.

The Datsun swerved back and forth, jumped the guardrail and plummeted down the cliff. It ricocheted off a large rock and came to rest in the shallow surf, leaving part of its roof and trunk exposed. Only a tiny section of the rear window remained in place.

The woman's body was pinned to the steering column, her arms hanging limply by her knees; shards of glass were embedded in her neck and face, and one temple of her sunglasses protruded from the left eye. Blood had spurted from a severed artery, matting her long hair.

"Christ, what a mess." The patrolman, careful to keep his highly polished boots from being scarred by the rough terrain, had finally reached the automobile and peered into the car's interior. He knew the woman was dead from the position of her body and from the smell of feces which was intensified by the hot day. He shoved away seagulls which had already gathered, waiting their chance to pick at the carcass.

"Uhhhh!" He took a deep breath and gazed down at the waves. Although he had seen hundreds of auto accidents, it always took him a minute to adjust to the carnage. As he made his way back to the top of the cliff, he could hear the siren of another patrol car pulling up to the accident scene.

"What you got, Joe?" The shift supervisor, a sergeant with gold chevrons on his sleeves, asked as he got out of the second car.

"A female jumped the cliff," Joe replied.

Cars were stacking up along the highway as a third patrol car pulled up, and the officers, with a windmilling of arms and batons, began marshalling onlookers onward. Huddled near the guard rail were several people, mostly tourists but also some native Californians who had decided to pull over and gawk. The shift supervisor approached the crowd, looking for witnesses to the accident. "Anyone see what happened here?" he queried.

For a minute no one moved; then two men walked slowly toward the sergeant. "Car just went off the road like a shot," the first man said. He was tall, with a receding hairline and dressed in the ubiquitous Bermuda shorts of all tourists. "This guy saw it, too."

"It was weaving for a spell and then, boom, it was gone over the edge. Didn't even slow down," the second man volunteered.

The supervisor could see that there were no skid marks. Perhaps the woman had been drinking. He climbed down the cliff face and, like the first patrolman, sniffed the air. No alcohol smell; no alcohol containers. Nothing. Perhaps a heart attack, but the woman was young.

"What you think?" Joe had again climbed down to the wreck.

"Beats me. Is the coroner on the way?"

"Yeah. I called while you were interviewing the witnesses."

The supervisor again scanned the auto. "We'll have to see if it was a malfunction in the brakes or something."

"Maybe she was an epileptic and had a seizure," Joe volunteered.

"Could be," the supervisor murmured. "Notice anything unusual?"

"What?" Joe responded.

"The back window. It's sort of cloudy."

"Yeah, that is odd. What do you suppose caused that?"

"Got me," the supervisor added, picking up a small piece of the frosted glass. "Are the other windows like this?"

"Hard to tell. They're scattered all over the cliff, but I'll take a look." Joe, careful not to slip on the wet rocks, began to pick his way around the car. "Here's another cloudy piece. Can't tell which window it came from, but it looks like maybe all the windows clouded up. Maybe that's why she crashed. Couldn't see out."

"Maybe, but she could just have rolled down the driver's window or pulled to the side of the road." The sergeant, his chevrons sparkling in the sun, scratched his head. "Well, we'll just have to wait and see what the coroner says."

"Is this the residence of Miss Tina Zabinski?"

Tina peered out the door at two police officers. She had taken a couple of Tylenol for a headache, had lain down and was not fully awake.

"Yes, I'm Tina Zabinski. Is something wrong?"

The two officers looked at each other and then back at Tina. Her answer was unexpected.

"You're Ms. Zabinski?"

"Yes, I'm Tina Zabinski." She emphasized her words, looking a little exasperated. "What's wrong?"

"I'm afraid there's been an accident, and the automobile is registered in your name.

"An accident! Oh, my God! Rhonda!" Tina exclaimed.

"I beg your pardon," the officer was puzzled.

"It's Rhonda! Rhonda! What time is it?"

"About 9 P.M." the younger officer replied, checking his watch. The woman was not very coherent. "Could you please tell us who was in your car?"

"Oh, my God!" Tina cried again. "It's Rhonda. Rhonda Schneider."

"Are you related to Miss Schneider?"

"No, I'm her roommate." Tina answered, in a calmer voice. "What hospital is she in? I'll just need a minute to get some clothes on... "

"Could we come inside, please?" The other officer interrupted. She was a short, dumpy female just past her mid-thirties and in an ill-fitting uniform.

"Uh, sure." Tina held the door for them. "Would you like to sit down?"

"Are you alone here?" the female inquired. Both officers remained standing.

"Right now, I am. But as I told you, Rhonda's my room-mate. Can't all of this wait? I need to get to the hospital."

"I'm afraid Miss Schneider is dead," the woman said.

"Dead! What do you mean dead? Rhonda went to my job. She's covering for me 'cause I've been sick." Tina knew there must be some mistake.

"The car she was driving left the road and she was killed." The male officer took Tina's arm and led her to a chair. "Is her family in town or can you give us a way to get in touch with them?"

Somehow Tina pulled herself together and gave the officers the necessary information, although she had a hard time remembering later on exactly what she had said. Rhonda's parents arrived the next day, and, although Tina had never met them before, she accompanied them first to the morgue and then to a funeral home. Arrangements were made to have Rhonda's body sent back to Phoenix for services and burial; her parents took any personal effects and indicated the rest should be donated to the Salvation Army. For Tina, who couldn't afford the airfare to Arizona for the funeral, it seemed as though everything was over and done with almost before she could realize Rhonda was gone.

When Todd returned from his trip, it was after midnight. It had been a profitable few days. Although he had not gone anywhere near Big Bear, he had visited several libraries and museums up and down the coast. He never tired of sitting in front of a Monet or a Renoir. Now, he could probably afford to purchase some expensive art works; however, this would not be a smart idea as he still needed to be very mobile. He could not become attached to anything that he couldn't simply abandon at a moment's notice.

The trip had also given him the opportunity to relax and over a couple of days to make the rounds of a cemetery where he had come up with several convincing names for future aliases when he needed them. He had wandered through the rows of headstones, searching for the names of children who had died young and at about the same time he had been born. This was fairly difficult, as most kids born in the fifties would live to a fairly ripe old age. He could look at dates as early as 1945 or as late as 1955. It would not be hard to appear to be younger or older within a ten-year range. He especially needed a birth date around 1942 for one of his proposed disguises.

Best of all, he had been able to compile a fairly extensive dossier on Charles Dylan. In addition to his short visit with Barbara Dylan, he had made a few discreet inquiries about Dylan at Pepperdine and learned that the professor had published several books dealing with crime and criminals and that Dylan occasionally was called in by police departments as a consultant. Sitting in on one of Dylan's lectures in the midst of nearly two hundred students, he found that the professor was a good lecturer, using examples to spice up his material, tossing in a bit of humor. Todd had been very attentive, watching the way Dylan moved, memorizing his facial details. You don't know me, Todd had thought as he left the lecture hall, but I'll remember you anywhere, Mr. Dylan.

Exhausted from the drive back to the beach house and the late hour, Todd immediately went to bed, planning to sleep in the next day. However, early the next morning, he was awakened by a banging on the door to his deck.

"Todd, Todd. Wake up"

He struggled into shorts, groped his way sleepily across the living room and opened the door.

"Tina!" Todd was stunned.

"Oh, Todd. Oh, it's been so awful. Oh, I wish you had been here. I was all alone when they told me. I just can't bear it." She literally threw herself into his arms.

"What? What?" Todd was confused. His mind raced back over the day that he left. What could have gone wrong? He had fixed it so Tina's car would produce fumes which would cause her to have an accident. Where was the car? Why wasn't Tina dead?

"Rhonda," Tina was now crying hysterically, clinging to Todd's neck.

"What about Rhonda? What are you saying?"

"She's dead! Oh, Todd, she's dead."

"Dead?" Todd couldn't believe what he was hearing. Rhonda, dead. "How? Stop crying, Tina." He shook her slightly. "Tell me what's happened."

It took a few minutes. Tina fished in her robe for a Kleenex and blew her nose loudly. Her face was a mess, puffy and red. Her hair was matted and looked like it hadn't been washed in days. She moaned softly as she sat down.

"A car wreck. She went off the Pacific Coast Highway and down a sharp incline almost into the water."

Todd still couldn't get the pieces to fit. He had seen Rhonda's car when he drove in the night before. It had not appeared to be damaged.

"But I saw Rhonda's car when I came home last night."

"Oh, it was my car. My car. It's totaled. I can't believe it happened. The police took it to the impound yard... to see why it went off the road."

"Your car?" Todd interrupted. The impound yard—he was immediately alert. Why not the junk yard? What had happened? "Why your car, Tina?"

"Well," Tina was more composed now. She produced a cigarette from her robe pocket and searched around for a light. Todd got up and got her a match. "Well," she began again, "remember the day you left?" She looked at him expectantly.

"Yeah."

"Well, I felt sick later on in the day. I think I had a bug. You know the kind. You get the trots, a little queasy. You know how it is; it comes on suddenly..."

"I get the picture," Todd broke in impatiently.

"So," Tina continued, looking somewhat hurt at his being so abrupt. "I asked Rhonda to cover for me because I had taken a couple of other days off—not thinking I would be sick—you know how that is."

Todd waited. Eventually she might get the story out.

"I have my own parking place; most of the help do as it gets so crowded. So I didn't want them to raise hell about a strange car being in my place. You know, our boss will tow people if someone parks in the lot who isn't using the restaurant."

"So what you're saying," Todd interjected hastily, "is that Rhonda was in your car when she had the accident and was killed."

"Yes, isn't it awful?"

It was awful, but not in the way Tina meant. Still, Todd murmured some words of condolence as he tried to think what to do next. He had not eliminated his problem with Tina who was constantly sticking her nose into his business and then spreading the information to anyone who would listen. He had not thought about the possibility that Rhonda would be driving Tina's car. That was the trouble. You could plan and plan perfectly, but you couldn't plan what other people would do. For just a moment he felt a twinge of guilt. He had liked Rhonda.

"What did the police say about the accident?" Todd asked. "Surely there must have been some sort of investigation?"

"Yes. The police came and talked to me three times. They kept asking about some residue or something like that on the windows. But I didn't know what they were talking about. And can you believe it? They said Rhonda suffocated. That's why she died—not from the wreck." Tina began to sniffle.

"So what's going to happen now?" Todd inquired, thinking a change of subject would stop the tears. "Will you be able to stay here at the beach?" He was hoping she would have to move out.

"Oh, I think so. How sweet of you to ask, but I won't be leaving you." Tina thought Todd was worried that she wouldn't be around anymore, and she was flattered by this misconception. "I'm still so shook up about everything that I haven't really had time to think. Larry and Jack said they'd help me out until I could get another roommate."

"Well, tell you what," Todd put his arm around her shoulder and moved her slowly toward the deck. He needed some time to get his thoughts together, but he didn't want to be too abrupt as he also might need more information from her. "You go and take a quick shower; I'll do the same and then we'll go and have an early breakfast at the Chart House. It will get your thoughts off of Rhonda. Okay?"

She smiled wanly. "Oh, it's nice to have you back, Todd. You're so understanding."

Yes, he thought, as he stood in his shower, I intend to be very understanding and vigilant. For the few days he still had to stay at the beach house, he would make Tina his constant companion whenever she was not working. In this way he could find out if the police were continuing to look into Rhonda's death; also he could ensure that Tina had little chance to mourn her roommate or to absent-mindedly mention that he was not really Todd Walker.

Because of the unfortunate mix-up and Rhonda becoming a victim instead of Tina, he knew it was now impossible to kill Tina. That would draw undue attention from the police—two deaths in the same house within such a short time span! The police would begin checking with the women's neighbors. He couldn't risk that happening. He would be gone shortly. Then, whatever Tina might suspect or say, it wouldn't matter.

THE MIAMI INTERLUDE

(OCTOBER 1981)

Within a few days Todd left L. A. although he had planned to remain there for at least another few weeks. Before going, he carefully cleaned the beach house and packed a light carry-on bag. The clothes which had made up Todd Walker's wardrobe would be left behind as they would no longer be needed, and if they were traced to Walker, what did it matter. Walker would no longer exist. All identification for Todd—driver's license, credit cards, bank statements, receipts—was consolidated and burned in the hibachi on the deck. He was slightly concerned as the credit cards emitted a toxic odor.

He retrieved from the garment bag in the closet the black wig, clothing and identification of his previous persona—Mark Proteus. The night before his flight, he left the beach house and took a room at the airport Marriott, registering as Proteus. That evening he spent with a rubber bathing cap on his head. He had poked small holes in it and pulled clumps of his bleached hair through the holes, just as he had seen them do for women in the local beauty shops. The protruding hair was then died black, giving him the appearance when the cap was removed of an older man with salt and pepper hair. The next morning, clad with the clothing worn by Mark Proteus when he arrived in L.A., the extra padding around his waist and wearing the carefully saved black wig, he returned his rental car to the airport and caught a shuttle to the terminal. Once he had gotten his boarding pass, he settled down to read the morning L. A. Times.

"Good morning," the stewardess greeted him as he boarded his plane. "Welcome to flight 307 to Miami. Your seat is number 3A in first class."

"Dylan?"

"Yes," Dylan replied in a gruff voice, cradling the telephone against his neck as he wiped greasy fingers on a paper towel. When Barbara called him to the phone, he had been working on his old Morgan, and he resented the interruption. One of Dylan's many interests was collecting and restoring classic automobiles, and Saturday morning was usually reserved for this activity. He now had parts strewn about the garage, making it impossible to park the family's Jeep Wagoneer and Ford LTD inside. Barbara Dylan was tolerant of his hobby, but she did have the habit of making snide remarks about their having a two-car garage which was really a parts store.

"This is Nolan at A. A. Cybertech."

"What can I do for you?" Dylan was surprised to hear from the man as it had been two months since he had given him a final report on the Bill Robinson disappearance.

"We've had some new information on Robinson or Proteus as you've nicknamed him. A call came in for him from a Santa Monica rental agency. Can you come down here?"

"Not for a few days." Dylan shifted the phone on his shoulder as he stared at the grease still caked under his fingernails and in the creases of his fingers. "I have some classes I simply can't cancel. However, I could be at your place early next Wednesday, if that's okay." He wondered what new information Cybertech could have gotten. Did this mean they wanted him to start the hunt for Robinson again? Was he willing to do this? The pay was good, he'd have to admit, but the chase certainly interfered with the rest of his life. Still, he was curious as to what new information had come up.

When he arrived at Cybertech headquarters, Dylan was immediately ushered into Nolan's office. "Good to see you," Nolan began after shaking his hand and making sure that Dylan was comfortably seated. "This call from a rental agency may be just what we need to track Robinson."

"So what do you want me to do?" asked Dylan. "Unless it's a really good lead, I think it will end up being nothing. And, what if I find him? I'm not a cop. I can't arrest him. Are you certain Vickers wants to invest more time and money in this venture?"

"I'm sure," Nolan replied with emphasis. He propped himself on the edge of the desk but leaned slightly forward. Dylan noted that the desk was highly polished oak but not nearly as large or fancy as Vickers'. "It's become a matter of pride with him. We may not ever press charges in order to avoid bad publicity, but Vickers simply wants him located."

"O. K. but it's going to take time and probably involve a great deal more money," Dylan responded as he got out a small notebook. "Tell me what was said."

"Well, one of our secretaries got a call last Friday asking for Robinson. Seems he rented a big beach home."

"How about getting the secretary in here?" Dylan asked.

A few minutes later Mrs. Davis appeared. "Nice to see you again, Mrs. Davis," Dylan greeted her, shaking the hand she offered. He noted that, as before when he had interviewed her, she was wearing a neat business suit, although her stiff demeanor was softened somewhat by a ruffle at the neck of her crisp, white blouse. "What did the rental agent say about Bill Robinson?"

"It was a complete surprise to me when this man called," Mrs. Davis began. "He asked to speak to Mr. Robinson. I didn't quite know what to do. So I stammered around a bit and finally said that Bill was not in the office right now. Could I help?" She waited but neither Dylan nor Nolan said anything.

"Well, the man told me that Mr. Robinson had rented a place on the beach just down from here in Santa Monica. But he didn't come back to get his refund on his initial deposit. It was almost a thousand dollars."

"Did the agent say when the place was rented?" Dylan queried.

"No, and I didn't think to ask. The man did say that Mr. Robinson had left some things behind at the house, and he needed to know what to do with them as he has other people moving into the place soon."

"You have the rental agent's name and address?"

"I have it," Nolan interrupted.

"So, that's all the agent said," Dylan asked Mrs. Davis.

"Yes, we didn't talk too long. I told him I'd get the

message to Mr. Robinson when he returned. I didn't really know what to say. I didn't want to mention that Mr. Robinson had been gone for months."

"Well, you did fine, Mrs. Davis. Thank you for talking with me." Dylan rose to signal that the meeting was over.

"O. K. I'm on my way to see the agent," Dylan said to Nolan. "This may be what we were hoping would turn up. I'll get back to you."

"Can you believe that guy," Nolan began as he walked with Dylan to the office door. "Renting a place here just a few miles away. What nerve."

"Yes, I guess no one can accuse him of not having nerve," Dylan responded with a slight smile. "But you've got to give him credit. He knew we wouldn't look for him right under our noses."

As he drove a short distance to the rental agent's office, Dylan went over the last few minutes' conversation. Now he was beginning to understand Proteus' plan.

"**M**r. Gomez, please," Dylan told the receptionist as he entered the foyer of Gomez Real Estate and Rental Agency, Inc. "I believe he's expecting me—Charles Dylan."

He glanced idly around as the woman pressed the intercom and announced him, her deep nasal voice in contrast to her dainty appearance. On the wall was a nicely framed poster showing California coastline and the words "location, location, location."

"Mr. Dylan. You're a friend of Mr. Robinson?" Gomez asked as they shook hands. He was almost as tall as Dylan but much heavier, and the Navy double breasted suit he wore only added to the impression of his being overweight. The office he led Dylan to was air-conditioned and well-furnished, with a desk of cherry wood and, in the corner, a beige leather sofa and chair. Dylan sat on the sofa.

"No, I've never met Mr. Robinson. I'm representing A. A. Cybertech, his employer. We have a problem. Mr. Robinson has disappeared."

"Disappeared? You mean he's been killed?" Gomez inquired.

"We don't know that. Actually, we don't know much. We hope you can help us. When did Robinson rent from you?"

"Let's see; he first talked with me in late February or early March and rented the house April 1. I remember specifically because he laughed and mentioned something about it being April Fools day. He paid the deposit and the last month's rent at that time."

"Did he pay by check or credit card?" Dylan asked.

"He paid by check, I think. I didn't worry about it being good since he said he wouldn't be moving in for a while."

"You wouldn't happen to remember if the check had his name on it or which bank it was drawn on, would you?"

"No. I'm sorry," Gomez shrugged and spread his hands. "I just didn't pay that much attention."

"No reason you should," Dylan replied, "especially since he wasn't moving in right away. Tell me, how much does the place rent for?"

"Well, it's not cheap. It's a beautiful place, great location, right on the beach, nice homes all around it. It rents for $2300 a month, more sometimes in the winter months when the northerners come down for the sun."

"That's a steep price all right."

"Well, yeah, I thought that, too. Especially when I saw that old Capri Robinson was driving." Gomez added. "But he didn't bat an eye at the price and coughed up the deposit right away."

So Robinson had been driving the Capri when he made the beach arrangements, Dylan mused. Apparently, he didn't care that Gomez saw the car because he knew he planned to dump it in airport parking at some later time.

"You told Cybertech's secretary that there were some things left at the house? Dylan asked. "What kind of things?"

"Yeah, there are some clothes, etc. I didn't make a list."

"Would it be O.K. with you if I went out and took a look?" Dylan wanted to know.

"Sure. In fact I'd like you to get the stuff out of there. I have new renters coming in next week." Gomez got up and so did Dylan. "What should I do about the deposit? It's a thousand and fifty dollars. I wouldn't have called Robinson's office if he had taken the house keys. I'd have kept the deposit and chalked it up to having new keys made and new locks installed, but since he left the keys inside, and I thought he might want to do business with me again, I thought I'd better get this matter cleared up properly."

Dylan deliberated for a minute. He remembered Margaret Robinson and her pathetic look. Still, if he had Gomez send the deposit back to her, she'd be very confused. "Just mail it back to his office at Cybertech," Dylan said as he started out the door and headed for the beach house.

t was a fancy place Dylan could see—trendy furniture, a good view of the waves. He opened the sliding glass door to the deck and aired out the place. Then he moved into the bedroom and checked the closet, picking through the clothing hanging there. No labels. Nothing extraordinary. Just the usual sport coat, some shorts, a faded pair of Levis and a few well-washed T-shirts. Hanging on a hook at the back of the clothes was a pair of red swimming trunks. He picked through the pockets of the sport coat. Nothing. Nothing in the Levis until he reached the small fifth pocket under the belt. He drew out a piece of paper—a neatly folded two-dollar bill.

"Bingo!" he exclaimed. So Bill Robinson had lived here, apparently since May when he disappeared. Smart fellow. Hide where they least expect you.

Stuck in the corner of the closet shelf, Dylan noticed a piece of paper. It turned out to be a small photograph of a bikini-clad, attractive woman with long, dark hair. No inscription. Dylan knew it wasn't Margaret Robinson. Was this why Proteus had embezzled the money and abandoned his wife?

"Helloooo." The screech came from the deck, startling Dylan.

"Yes," he replied as he walked back toward the open door.

"Oh, I thought Todd had returned."

"Uhh, not that I know of."

"I'm Tina Zabinski. Are you my new neighbor then?" Tina insisted, examining him from head to toe.

"No, I'm checking into a missing person report. Who is this Todd?"

"Todd Walker—the man who lived here all summer. Actually he wasn't Todd Walker at all. His real name was Anthony Stevens. Is he the one you're checking on? Is he missing? Is this about the divorce?"

Anthony Stevens. Dylan remembered that name from information Cybertech had supplied to him. "Did you know Todd, or Anthony, well?"

"I thought I did, but he just up and left a couple of weeks ago. He didn't even say goodbye to me," Tina said unhappily. "I thought maybe he had to go back to Boston about his divorce."

"Divorce?"

"Yes, his wife was getting a divorce, and he was out here trying to keep her from finding him and his money," Tina replied. "Or maybe he had to see his publisher. But you said he's missing?"

"Publisher?" Dylan wanted to get her mind off the idea that someone was missing.

"Yes, he was a writer. Didn't you know?"

"No, I don't have that in my notes." Dylan replied.

"Did he let you read his work, or did he ever say what he was writing about?"

"Well, I guess he never really told us. He was here for several months, and then one day he just wasn't."

"Us?" Dylan questioned.

"Friends of mine. Todd came to several of my parties, but he wasn't too good a mixer. He never talked much about himself." By now Tina had worked her way into the house and settled comfortably on the rattan sofa. She teasingly crossed her legs, making sure her white poplin skirt was well above her knees.

"I'm not trying to be offensive..." Dylan paused for a moment, glancing at her tanned legs, "but I need to know if you and Walker were....involved."

"Well, if you mean were we sleeping together," Tina tried to look coy, "we weren't. Not that I wasn't hoping, mind you. Todd was really pretty good looking. All of the girls said so. He was just so yummy; he reminded you of Robert Redford; he was just, just...."

"So what are you saying?" Dylan interrupted as tactfully as he could.

"Wellll, he just never seemed to be interested. I dropped a few hints, and he was attentive. He explained that until he got his divorce, he just didn't want to get involved. He seemed to prefer to be alone a lot. He stayed by himself a great deal. Of course, he was writing; I did mention that, didn't I?" Tina began curling a strand of hair around her finger.

"So you only saw him as a neighbor?"

"Mostly, but he did take me out quite a few times for dinner on my nights off. I work most nights, you know.

And, he usually came over if I invited him. That's why I can't believe he would just go off without at least saying goodbye. I thought we were good friends." Tina stopped talking and gazed off toward the ocean.

"Could you give me more of a description of Todd Walker? Maybe we're not talking about the same man." Dylan wanted to get Tina's mind off of Todd having abandoned her.

"Let's see. He was tall, taller than me by a lot." Tina held her hand over her head. "But not quite as tall as you, I think." Tina stood up and moved close to Dylan to compare heights. "He was very good looking as I said, with blue eyes and the blondest hair. Good shape. Jogged every morning, but then he smoked a pipe. Seems funny, doesn't it. Jogged for his health and then smoked?"

Dylan made no reply, so Tina continued her rambling. "But very quiet, sort of withdrawn, like I said. Didn't seem to like to talk much. The strong, silent type, I guess."

"Do you know where he was from?" Dylan felt he was hearing the same thing over and over. She talked but didn't say anything. He wondered what Walker's feelings might have been for this woman. Did he like her? Did he only tolerate her?

"Well, I'm sure he said Boston. I have an uncle living there, and we talked about that. Or maybe it was Florida; he talked about Florida quite a bit. Said he really liked warm weather. That's why he had come here to do his writing."

"Do you remember when he rented the place?"

"Oh, I don't think he rented it. Someone else must have rented it for him. At least I remember seeing another man here a couple of times at night. I try to keep tabs on what is going on."

"I'll just bet you do," Dylan thought. If Todd Walker had made the mistake of telling this woman anything that was really true, she probably latched on to it and repeated it to anyone who would listen. When his thoughts returned to Tina, she was still babbling.

"I thought that other man had rented it. Then Todd just suddenly appeared one Saturday morning on the beach. I greeted him as I wanted to be neighborly. I remember because we had a big party that night, and he came over and met the gang."

"The other man. What did he look like?"

Tina thought for a moment, obviously confused by the question. "Oh, you mean the man I saw before I saw Todd. He was fairly tall also with brown hair, I think. Nothing much stands out. Really plain looking, but, of course, I didn't really get a good look as it was usually getting dark when I saw him. I guess I should have been neighborly."

"Definitely the Bill Robinson identity," Dylan thought. Robinson had rented the place prior to his disappearance, had everything set up. He must have been planning this for some time. Changed his identity, really covered his tracks well. He wondered if Robinson would have rented the place had he known earlier about Tina.

"Is there anything else you can tell me about Todd Walker? Did he have any visitors? Did you see anyone else with him? What did he do all day? Did he work anywhere?"

"Goodness, you do ask a lot of questions," Tina laughed as she sat down again. "I told you he was a writer. I guess he wrote all day; that's what he said he did. I work nights, so I don't know if he had any other friends."

"Did he drive a car?"

"Oh, yes. A spiffy red convertible."

"You don't happen to know the license, do you?"

"Heavens no. I can't remember my own license number." Tina giggled.

"Would you say Walker was a good neighbor?" Dylan asked abruptly. It seemed to take forever to glean the pertinent information about Walker from the woman's drivel. "Never had any trouble with him, did you?"

"Oh, heavens no. In fact he was very kind and considerate. I don't know what I would have done without him after my roommate was killed. I had a hard time dealing with that, and Todd was so good to me, just stayed close every minute."

"Roommate killed? You didn't mention a roommate. How was she—or he—killed?"

"Well, it was very sad and so unexpected. Just like something you read about or see in the movies. You know? Where fate steps in and the unexpected happens."

Tina waited for Dylan to comment. When he didn't, she continued.

Well, Rhonda—that was her name, Rhonda—had driven my car instead of hers and went off the highway and over a cliff. She was dead instantly. It was just fate that I wasn't driving that afternoon. Just simply fate."

"Was she speeding?"

"No. The police couldn't explain why it happened. There was apparently some problem with her breathing. I think they said she suffocated."

"In the car?" That didn't make sense. Dylan was trying to fit the pieces into a whole puzzle.

"Well, that's what the police said. They questioned me several times, as if I'd done something to cause the accident."

"So, it was ruled an accident?"

"Yes. The only thing the police ever said was that there was some kind of queer stuff on the windows, almost like they were frosted." Tina stopped and shrugged. "But this all happened in September. We don't have frost even in the winter." She looked helplessly at Dylan, as if he would have the answer.

"That is puzzling." Dylan replied. For a few moments they both sat in silence.

"Well, you've been very helpful." Dylan felt he had gotten all of the information, important and not, he could from Tina and wanted to get away from the chattering woman. "If I think of anything else, I'll stop back by. Oh," he suddenly stopped, retrieving from his pocket the photograph he had found in the bedroom. "Do you think this could be a picture of his wife?"

"Oh, my God! That's Rhonda. She's wearing my bathing suit." Tina was suddenly overcome with grief and began sobbing. "Where did you get this?"

Dylan debated whether he should answer her question but decided it was okay to do so. "It was among Walker's possessions, some that are still here."

Tina stopped crying. "He had her picture? I didn't know she was seeing him, actually dating him. She never told me." Tina looked indignant. "Can you believe it? My own roommate. Well I never! That's probably why he left the day after I told him about the accident. I'll bet they were romantically involved—right behind my back."

Dylan was sorry that he had mentioned the photo. It was of no help in his investigation and now he had an angry Tina to placate. "He probably had a photo of both of you, and probably took yours with him," Dylan murmured, hoping this would soothe her damaged ego.

Finally he was able to usher Tina out the sliding door, lock the place and proceed toward his car. Where could Proteus, or Todd, as he now was calling himself have gone? Did he go to Boston, since he had mentioned that city to Tina. Perhaps Florida. Or is he still here in town? You had to admire the guy's cleverness, Dylan conceded, although he hated to admit that he was stumped.

"Yoo hoo. Wait a minute." Tina ran after Dylan. "I just remembered I have this photo of Todd." She handed him a Polaroid snapshot. "Larry took shots of all of us at one of my parties. Todd just happened to be in this one with me, although he was never much for having his picture taken."

"I'll bet he wasn't," Dylan thought examining the photo. It was a good, clear snapshot of Tina, a big smile pasted on her face, and of a handsome male in the background. If one colored the man's blonde hair brown and took away the California tan, Dylan thought, it could be a photo of Bill Robinson. Obviously, there was no longer a Robinson nor, probably, a Todd Walker. Proteus had changed identities again. He would bet his life on it.

"Sure you don't want to keep this?" Dylan asked.

"Are you kidding?" Tina snapped. "I hope I never see or hear from him again." Tossing her head, she flounced back toward her house.

As he drove away from Tina, Dylan let his thoughts continue to wander. Another car accident involving people who knew Proteus. That made three—the father, the Air Force co-worker and now the neighbor. To Dylan that was one too many coincidences. Proteus must have been involved in all three, and the death of Rhonda, with its police involvement, was why he had vacated his beach hideout so suddenly. But why kill Rhonda? He might have to come back and question Tina further. He hoped not; he felt that he had gotten all the information she could give him. Still, Tina had thought the world of Todd Walker until the Rhonda photo surfaced. She had believed everything he told her. Amazing, wasn't it how people just took others at face value? Never questioned anything. No wonder things could happen to people without anyone knowing—or caring it seemed. Certainly Tina had discovered that Todd Walker was an alias, that apparently he was actually Anthony Stevens, and yet she was willing to become his bed partner. No fear of anything bad happening to her. Dylan shook his head. Strange world.

Dylan drove down the beach and into a Jack in the Box, the nearest fast-food place he could find. He hated fast food, but he didn't have time to spend at a regular restaurant. He ordered a cheeseburger, fries and a Diet Coke and sat under one of the faded striped umbrellas that covered the concrete table and bench, casually watching the continuous ribbon of traffic as it wound its way along the coast. Nearby were some droopy marigold plants in plastic containers. The establishment, like the food, was not too appetizing.

Where to go next, he thought. Probably the car rental place but which one? May as well start with the airport as Walker would probably have flown out—if he left town. That was the problem. He was only guessing that Walker had left town. He could have simply moved just up the beach. Like he had done the first time, that would be the smart thing to do.

Dylan took a long sip of the Coke and admired the rear of a scantily clad eighteen-year-old lifeguard who was climbing back onto her watchtower. Would he have left town as Walker? He didn't fly back to L.A. as Walker. So he could have come up with any number of aliases. Dylan sighed. But, maybe he used the name of Mark Proteus as he did last May. Careless of him if he did so. Of course Proteus had ceased to exist when Robinson became Walker, so that might be the case this time. Talk about confusing!

By now Dylan was finished with the burger and most of the fries. Tossing the remains in the trash can, he headed for the airport. He'd check out the car rental first and then return home to see if he could locate the old flight manifests.

At LAX Dylan approached all of the car rental agencies, explaining to each one that he needed to know if a Todd Walker, a Bill Robinson or an Anthony Stevens had returned a car within the last month. If, as Tina had said, Walker had an auto the whole time he was at the beach house, he must have rented it. Surely, he wouldn't have bought a car and then simply abandoned it. Of course, he could have bought a car and driven anywhere. However, Dylan was gambling that he hadn't. The rental agencies promised that they would get him as much information as possible within a few weeks. It was their busy time, and that was the best they could do.

Dylan appreciated the drive home. It gave him time to think. Tina had said Florida or Boston, but she had also mentioned that Todd Walker liked warm weather. As a young man in Minnesota before he began his life of hiding, Joshua Petersen had left that cold country and never returned. He had not remained in Colorado either when he left the military. Boston was unlikely. A warm climate, Dylan thought. That's where Walker would go.

Of course, that left Phoenix, Galveston, New Orleans, San Antonio, and Houston, just to name a few. Maybe he'd go back to Houston. The trail had grown cold there. The way Walker's mind worked was not ordinary. Originally he had returned to hide in L.A., and no one had suspected him to do so. Now who would think he would return to Houston where he had disappeared?

Walker had rented an expensive beach house and rented or bought a rather conspicuous auto. Would he continue to do this? When he was Robinson, he had gone out of his way to be inconspicuous. Dylan's head hurt. He needed to see if Walker had left L.A. or was still in the area. Maybe if he got the car rental information, Proteus might appear on one of them. If not, maybe he would get lucky with recent airline manifests.

It took three weeks before Dylan began to get lists from the rental agencies. Sitting at his desk with the French doors to the garden slightly ajar, he began the boring task of reviewing the material. From outside he could hear a lonesome cricket chirping. Fragrance from freshly cut grass drifted into the room, and he longed to be outside instead of in the study.

The first four were of no help, but Avis showed that a Mustang convertible had been returned by one Todd Walker on October 19th. It had been a long-term rental, almost six months to be exact, to the tune of nine hundred bucks a month. "Wow!" Dylan said. Then he began to wonder. Why wouldn't the rental agency have thought this odd? Over five thousand dollars for a rental car. He called Avis and questioned this issue. The explanation was simple. Walker had renewed the rental each month. It was not unusual for some businessmen to rent a car for several weeks at a time. Besides, it was not always the same agent who handled the transaction. "Avis was in the business of renting cars," he was told, "not questioning the clients about their usage."

Well, at least Dylan was pretty sure of one thing. Walker had flown away. Now he would request passenger manifests for the day and several days immediately after the auto was returned and see if Mark Proteus or any of his other aliases would appear.

After he had shed the garb of Mark Proteus in the Miami airport men's room and changed into new clothing which he had carried on the airplane, Todd had divorced himself from all of his past aliases. Bill Robinson was gone; Todd Walker was gone; now, even Proteus was gone. He emerged in an expensive tan gabardine suit—a middle-aged Cuban with horn-rimmed glasses and a cane.

"I reserved a four-door Chevrolet," he explained to the young woman behind the Hertz counter. "My name is Hector Pentojas."

Shortly thereafter he was on his way to a complex near Hialeah Race Track where, under the name of Mark Proteus, he had rented an efficiency apartment a year ago when he had been in Miami on business for Cybertech. He had hated to pay the rent for the past year, but he always kept an escape route handy. Now it was being put to good use.

The following morning Hector made the rounds of the automobile dealerships. He needed a fairly impressive car to fit his new image and had transferred a substantial amount of money into a new bank account. Finally, he decided on a dark blue Cadillac Seville, its dove gray leather interior and cassette player adding an aura of opulence. He had the papers made out in the name Pentojas, returned his rental car and took a cab back to pick up his Caddie. The dealer had wanted him to finance the auto, but he quickly explained that he was not willing to pay finance charges and had provided a certified check for the full price. His next task would be to purchase a home and move out of the apartment as soon as possible. Any trail would stop there with Mark Proteus. Like Robinson and Walker, Proteus would simply have vanished.

Buying a house was a time-consuming business, but a house provided more privacy than an apartment building or condominium. Fortunately, he had looked at various locations in the Miami area on previous business trips, so he knew where he would like to live. After three weeks of trudging through various homes, he made an offer on a fairly expensive Spanish style bungalow at 27360 Nightingale Avenue—a prestigious area but not the top of the line. With all of the money he had accumulated so far, he could afford to buy any house he wanted in the most upscale neighborhood, but he knew he should purchase a more modest abode that would fit in with the image of a professional man—one who was successful but not overly affluent.

"Will Mrs. Pentojas be joining you soon?" the female realtor inquired as she showed him through the spacious rooms, several of which had vaulted ceilings and ceiling fans. The white walls had been recently painted, and the

Spanish tiles on the floor gave the rooms an old-world appearance. It had several features that Hector particularly liked—recessed lighting, a large separate dining room, a well-equipped kitchen and a swimming pool to the right of a cement patio surrounded by tall hedges.

"I'm a widower," Pentojas replied.

"Oh, I'm so sorry," the realtor looked away. "Perhaps this house is too large for you, then, with its four bedrooms and three baths."

"No. It's just about right. I occasionally have to do some entertaining for my business."

"You said your were a consultant?"

"That's correct. I consult with large firms in regard to computer programming, marketing, etc."

"And you're just moving to Miami?"

"I have business interests worldwide, but I decided since my wife died to settle in Miami. I like the warm weather."

Hector's offer was accepted; he surreptitiously moved his clothes out of the rented apartment and began the laborious job of furnishing his new home. Setting up an office in one of the smaller bedrooms, he purchased a word processor, advertised for and hired a housekeeper who would come Monday through Friday to clean, do laundry and prepare an evening meal, if he were not going to be dining out.

All of this had taken no more than five weeks, and he gloated over how smoothly his plans had run and how easy it all had been. He was very comfortably settled in his home, had more than enough funds to get his new scam underway and had eluded the guy, Dylan, who had been looking for Robinson or Walker. Sitting on the patio late one evening, he smiled contentedly. Hector Pentojas was safe!

"Bingo!" Dylan shouted after hours of pouring over the American Airlines manifest. There on a Miami-bound flight was the name Mark Proteus. "I was right after all about his destination."

Two days later Dylan was in Miami and immediately checked the car rental agencies. No Mark Proteus had rented an auto within the past several months.

So the trail stops here, Dylan thought. The guy could have merely changed planes and gone anywhere. Of course, if he had stayed in Miami, he would need a hotel room, unless he had friends or relatives with whom he could stay. Dylan spent four days on the phone, calling several luxury hotels. Proteus was not the type of guy to stay in a dive if the beach house was any indication. No Mark Proteus or any of the other aliases appeared on any register.

Depressed and tired, Dylan called Barbara. "It's over."

"You found him?" Barbara said excitedly.

"No, I've lost him. He's just vanished again."

"There are no leads?"

"Nothing on a car rental; nothing on any Mark Proteus

or Bill Robinson or Anthony Stevens or Todd Walker at any of the hotels or motels or leaving on any airline." Dylan gave a long sigh. "I've had it. He must have moved on to another city from here."

"But if he didn't leave Miami," Barbara interjected, "he'd have to have some place to live."

"I've been thinking along those lines. Perhaps he knows someone here. If that's the case, it is over." Dylan stated. "On the other hand, since he had a house ready and waiting for him in L.A. when he switched to Walker, he may have done the same here. I guess I'll give it one more try and check apartment rentals."

"That's a good idea," Barbara encouraged him.

"But he could be anybody. He could be in the room right next to me, and I wouldn't know it. He could rent a place under the name of Ronald Reagan. Remember, he's like a chameleon. He changes identities like the lizard changes colors. Checking apartment rentals is an insurmountable task."

Still, the next day Dylan began to check. Weeks went by. Many people refused to cooperate. Some came up with the name Robinson or Walker, but those were fairly common names and none turned out to be the one he wanted. He finally expanded his search out of the immediate Miami area. After a month and a half, Dylan literally stumbled across an economy-sized apartment that had been rented by a Mark Proteus. However, the manager of the small apartment complex said he had seen Proteus only once. "The rent was paid on time, but no one lived in the place."

"Didn't you think this was odd?" Dylan asked.

"Well, hell yeah! But as long as I got my money, who cares. Saved wear and tear on the place. I got no complaints."

"So Proteus never lived here?"

"Yeah. He did. For just a few days about two months ago. But I hardly ever saw him, only saw that the lights were on at night."

"What did he look like?" Dylan persisted.

"Near as I can remember he was an older guy. Had glasses and always carried a cane."

"Don't suppose he gave you a forwarding address?"

"No. In fact he didn't even tell me when he was leaving. The rent was paid up until the end of the month, but he must have left some time during one night. I didn't see him leave. I didn't see lights in the place again. I do remember he parked a blue Cadillac out front of his place."

"A Cadillac?" Dylan was suddenly alert. "Is that what most of your tenants drive?"

The manager laughed. "Not really. I doubt if the guy owned it; the bank did. A lot of people drive cars they can't afford."

That was true, Dylan thought, but not Proteus. Money was not a problem for Proteus. Dylan sighed. He would check out the Cadillac dealers, but he already knew the car would be registered under some name other than those Proteus had used before; the lead would stop there. Vickers and Nolan were not going to find their thief. As far as Dylan was concerned, Proteus was gone for good.

Hector Pentojas signed the receipt for the last delivery of furniture which he had purchased to fill his new home. Nearby was the Diplomat Presidential Golf Course which gave the area a sense of spaciousness. Interstate 95 provided him with immediate motor access in and out of town, just in case this would be needed quickly, and the airport was within twenty minutes.

Closing the door behind him he crossed the Spanish tiles into the large living room and made his way past a rather pretentious wet bar to the patio. He looked with satisfaction around the well-landscaped yard, noting the tall palms with their branches clattering in the breeze. Near the stone wall surrounding the grounds, was a lemon tree, and he could imagine the sweet odor when it bloomed in the early spring. The grass had just been recently mowed and edged, and as he settled himself for a few minutes of relaxation on the chaise lounge, he said, "Sure beats the hell out of Duluth!"

After a few minutes, Pentojas wandered back into the house surveying his new beige leather couch and chair. In the dining room a large glass table with six chairs and a credenza sat starkly against one wall. This will never do, Pentojas thought. I need to find me a decorator who will get this place in shape. I simply don't have the time or the motivation to move furniture and hang pictures. He had done all of that type of work when he had been married to Margaret.

Shortly before noon the next day Hector opened the door to an attractive middle-aged woman. "Mr. Pentojas," the woman peered at him through large dark glasses. She had on a bright yellow suit with a blouse covered in large aqua blossoms. "I'm Georgette De Angelo."

"Oh, yes, Ms. De Angelo. Please come in." Hector led the way into the living room, noting an almost overpowering scent of roses as the woman drifted past him. "Do I need to show you around?"

"Well, yes, it would help, although I can see why you called me." The woman moved slowly in a circle, surveying not only the living room but the dining area and the patio beyond. "You do need a lot done to make this place habitable. This is just atrocious, so plain... so ungarnished."

Pentojas nearly laughed as he followed her through the home. Georgette was anything but ungarnished. Her platinum hair was swept up in large curls on top of her head and pinned with a silver barrette. Long silver earrings glinted in the light, and a squash blossom necklace, accented with large turquoise stones, ringed her neck. Bright red toenails peeked out of her high-heeled yellow sandals.

"You really have some great potential here, Mr. Pentojas. The rooms are spacious and the light is good practically everywhere. Some art objects and a little color would just do wonders for this place. You wouldn't recognize it." Hector hoped by color she didn't mean yellow and turquoise as he thought that might be too much garnish.

"I was thinking about some good paintings," Hector offered. "Not a Van Gogh, of course." They both chuckled. "But maybe something contemporary, a good quality print. I am very interested in art."

"Well, do you wish me to just use my own judgment?"

"I suppose that would be best. Nothing too ostentatious. Just something a middle-aged bachelor could be comfortable in," Hector said. "Now, can you start right away, and do I need to give you a deposit up front?"

"I'll get right to it. If possible, I would like around $5,000 to start with, if you can manage that at this time."

"Certainly. Please come back into my office, and I'll write a check."

Hector led the way to his desk, got out a checkbook and began writing. As she took the check from his hand, Georgette inquired as to the nature of his employment.

"Computers," Pentojas replied. "I am a computer expert."

It did not take Hector long to "get connected" in Miami—five months, but that was not long when one was setting up a new business and seeking clients. First he took a lease on an office on 75th Street, just a few blocks away from the John F. Kennedy Causeway. It was ample in size, conveniently divided with a separate area for his receptionist/secretary. The building had only recently been completed, but was rapidly filling up. He felt fortunate to get the lease, not only because the premises were pristine but because the other occupants were also new. In this way, he would not be the "new guy on the block," so would not arouse the curiosity of others.

This would be his home base. If everything went as he had planned, he could be here for several years, hopefully a life time. Therefore, he needed an office which would be comfortable and would also be impressive enough to show perspective clients that he was successful. With the aid of Georgette De Angelo, the office was set up. Shopping at several antique stores, the two acquired an intricately carved desk of teak which he was assured had been made in the 1600s in Thailand. A large white sofa with pale green wing chairs nestled in one corner. Watercolor landscapes, which the decorator had purchased from an artist at a local gallery, provided a soothing ambience.

After completing the office decor, Pentojas had H. P. Consulting placed on a bronze plaque on the lobby marquee. Then, he called an employment agency and quickly selected thirty-six-year-old Sharon Gleason to run the place. Mrs. Gleason, the wife of a dentist, projected the image of the typical suburban housewife—modestly attired with unremarkable features and dishwater blonde hair. She was eager to get the position as her two boys were in school all day, and she was bored with little to do. In addition, the hours Hector quoted her—nine A.M. to 4 P.M. four days a week—were very attractive.

Her primary duties would be to answer the telephone, schedule appointments, take care of the billing of client fees, and handle correspondence. In other words, Sharon would manage the legitimate portion of the business. Eventually, this client base would be comprised of twenty-seven fairly large companies, within five of which Pentojas was implementing a small embezzlement scheme without Gleason or the companies aware of his activities.

Several of the consulting contacts had been arranged prior to his move to Miami. From these he secured references and gradually made additional contacts. Ms. De Angelo spoke to one of her friends who hired him for a small job. Then that client spoke to another firm, praising Hector for his expertise. One thing led to another. Business computers were the wave of the future, and someone with the experience Hector had was in great demand. Before he knew it, he was a busy man. Through one of the contacts, he was referred as a consultant to Miami Utilities, Inc. This had been his prime objective—a public utility or another large corporation similar to Cybertech—and he had finally reached it. Within a few weeks he had signed a contract to implement a new billing program for the company and to be on call for any of their other computer needs or problems which might arise.

The greater Miami population was nearly three million. Pentojas had decided to add to each electric bill a measly nineteen cents a month which would net him roughly five hundred seventy thousand a month or a yearly total of six million eight hundred forty thousand. Just nineteen cents. No one would ever notice. How many people checked their monthly electric bills that closely? For that matter how many people knew how to calculate the meter readings? This would add nicely to his already ample nest egg.

From his legitimate side of the business he was raking in over ninety thousand a year which paid the office expenses and the bills at home. He was living well—but not too well. He constantly reminded himself not to draw too much attention to his lifestyle.

The months passed quickly. He became a member of the neighboring golf club. He dined out frequently, especially on the weekends. Now and then he entertained in his home—clients and their wives—who were always impressed with the decor. Ms De Angelo had been a good investment.

Once in a while, he invited a woman to a concert or out to dinner—a widow who played golf at the club, the friend of a client who lacked an escort. He was in great demand as a slightly older, eligible bachelor with, obviously, a good business and a bright future. However, he dated infrequently, and he always made it clear to the women that he was not looking for any long-term entanglements. When anyone questioned why he didn't marry, and Georgette De Angelo did this frequently, he always looked rather dejected and said, "Well, I would. I really would, if I could just meet the right woman."

At least four times a year he took a brief vacation to Europe, always unaccompanied. In this way he was able to set up accounts in which to transfer the monthly utility money. He always indicated, if anyone asked him, that he had combined a little business with pleasure.

Occasionally someone would inquire into his past, but he had planned a good cover story. Yes, he was Cuban. Well, part Cuban. His American mother had married a Cuban lawyer, and he had been born in Cuba where the family had lived until shortly before Fidel Castro took over; then his parents and he had fled to Miami. However, already ill with cancer, his mother had died within a few months. He had been sent to Minnesota to live with his mother's sister and her physician husband. The couple was childless and eager to have their nephew stay until his father could get resettled. "That never happened," Hector would say, looking sadly at the floor. "My father was killed in an automobile accident."

If questions were raised about his schooling or his previous work, he also had prepared answers. He had first gone to college in Minnesota but migrated to the West Coast and graduated from the University of Oregon. He had worked in computer programming there and in neighboring states before getting into his own consulting business. Finally, he had decided to move to Miami as he always remembered it fondly, even though his stay there as a young boy had been so brief.

If anyone queried him about his military service, he would merely shrug and point to his cane. The slight limp he had perfected was explained as an injury to his hip while attempting to play college football.

For four years he had no problems. His cover was sound; his finances were in excellent shape and growing ever larger; his feeling of being safe and secure increased daily. He reveled in the semi-tropical climate. Truly, Miami had been a good choice, and he planned to make it a permanent home.

Dylan had finally given up the chase. It killed him to do so. Until now he had never failed in tracking down a culprit or solving a case, and he had worked on quite a few for various police departments around the country. He settled back into teaching classes at Pepperdine, but the case of the mysterious Bill Robinson continued to nag him. He had even worked up a case study based on Proteus and used this as a semester project for his graduate students, hoping one of them might come up with something he had overlooked. He simply couldn't get Proteus off his mind.

"What are you doing up at this time? It's almost 3:00 o'clock. Are you ill?" Barbara Dylan walked into the den, tying the sash of her pink velour robe as she spoke.

"No," Dylan replied. "Just can't sleep."

"You seem so restless all the time lately. I could hear you pacing up and down. What's bothering you?"

"Nothing I can really put my finger on." Dylan moved toward the door. "How about something to drink? Coffee? Tea? Something stronger?"

"Coffee, I guess. I'm not sure I can get back to sleep now anyway. But let me make it. Your coffee is always so strong it can walk out of the cup." She followed him into the kitchen and began to fill the glass coffee pot.

Dylan got two mugs from the cupboard and settled himself on a stool at the tiled counter. The pungent aroma of coffee grounds filled the air as Barbara removed a canister lid.

"Barb," he began.

"Ummm," she mumbled as she reached into the refrigerator for some cream.

"What would you think about me calling Bart Bensenberg—about the Proteus case?"

"Your old Marine buddy? I thought they only handled kidnappings."

"You've been watching too many TV shows," Dylan chided her. "The F.B.I. gets involved in all kinds of things."

"Then why didn't Cybertech call them in when you were first investigating?" Barbara placed a blue linen napkin and spoon in front of Dylan.

"They didn't want the publicity," Dylan explained patiently. "Vickers wanted that money loss kept as quiet as possible. I'm not sure even today that the police know money was stolen."

"Well, I think that's silly. How can anyone apprehend a criminal if they don't know a crime has been committed?"

"I agree," Dylan rubbed the back of his neck and stretched slightly. "But it's their company and their stockholders who are kept in the dark. I promised I would be very discreet." Dylan stressed the word "very."

Barbara poured the steaming coffee into Dylan's mug and set it before him. "Well, call Bart. You don't have to ask my permission," she said as she filled her cup. "I don't know what he can tell you, but it would be nice to know how he's doing."

I t took nearly two weeks for Agent Bartholomew Oliver Bensenberg to return Dylan's call. He had been out of the office, he explained, but was very glad to hear Dylan's voice on his answering machine when he had returned.

Dylan could picture Bensenberg from their days together in the Marine Corps. Five foot nine inches of a well-muscled body topped by dark hair and hazel eyes above a prominent nose, Bensenberg could have posed for a recruiting poster. He had seen action in the Vietnam War and had a purple heart tucked away somewhere in his Marine souvenirs. When he walked, people could tell by the sound of his heels resonating on the floor that Bensenberg was a man in control—a leader. He was unmarried, a perfectionist who gave excessive attention to detail. In his desk he kept a brush so that his suit was always spotlessly free of any small piece of lint. The F.B.I. as an organization loved him; his co-workers hated him as he always made them look rather tacky by comparison.

The two men exchanged pleasantries for a few minutes,

catching up on each other's lives. Bensenberg inquired about Barbara and the children. Dylan commented that he had recently read that Bensenberg had been promoted to Special Agent.

"Bart, I need a big favor," Dylan finally began, "and I'm not certain you can help me out."

"Hey, what's a Marine for if not to help out another Marine?" Bensenberg laughed loudly.

While the F.B.I. man listened patiently, Dylan explained his problem with the Bill Robinson case. "I've given him the name Proteus since he keeps changing on me," Dylan explained. Carefully he went over each step he had taken as he tried to trace Proteus and his various aliases across the country.

"I have this gut feeling he's in the Miami area, Bart, but it's just a feeling. I haven't a thing to go on except he did fly in there."

"Well, I'm not sure I can help you," Bart began. "Let me think a minute. You say this Cybertech never reported the crime?"

"No! I'm certain they didn't. And you can't say anything about it. This is a confidential matter."

"Okay!" Bensenberg's voice shot up a notch. "Well, in that case, let me do some quiet checking around. However, unless this guy—what did you call him, Proteus?—does something like this again and we do get called in, he may have just gotten away clean."

"I know, but I can't seem to shake him. He keeps me up nights, trying to think as he would think. Barbara's about to divorce me."

"He'd have to do something where we could get called

in," Bensenberg added thoughtfully, repeating what he had already stated. "Something where federal funds would be involved or funds taken across a state line. Something like that."

"Okay," Dylan said, "but I guess I need to mention something else. I suspect that Proteus not only stole a great deal of money, I think he may have killed a couple of people. One I'm almost sure of—a guy he knew in the air force who might have gotten on to him. The guy died in an auto accident which may not have been an accident. Also, when he was a teenager, his father was killed in an auto accident that was sort of suspicious. I think he did in his old man."

"Hey, that is good to know. Still, he'd have to murder someone where we'd be called in. Seems to me the embezzling is his chief activity."

"Well, keep your ears and eyes open," Dylan concluded. "You never know when you might hear of something or make some small connection."

"Will do, and I'll be sure to call you if anything turns up. But," and Bensenberg emphasized the word, "don't get your hopes up. I doubt if you ever hear of Mr. Proteus, or whatever his name is, again."

Bensenberg was probably right, Dylan thought, as he hung up the phone and leaned back in his desk chair. And whoever Proteus is now, if I were he, I'd have left the country long ago.

Fall 1985

I t was an unusually warm day for November, Hector noted, as he made his way into the Miami Utilities building. After a pleasant lunch of broiled halibut and a salad laced with feta cheese, Hector had decided to wrap up his day by installing the remainder of a new software program. Riding up in the elevator he chatted with one of the clerks who worked in receiving.

For over three years Hector had been hired as a consultant for the utility. He was in and out of the place several times a month—sometimes several times a week, depending on the job—so a small office had been set aside for his use. He was just settling in at the computer terminal when a loud pop followed shortly by a shriek brought him to his feet. Quickly he moved toward the door and peered into the hall.

"Get an ambulance," a male voice ordered from an office a few doors away. Immediately a female ran to a nearby phone and began to dial.

"Oh, my God," another female voice shrilled. "Oh, noooo.!" A male employee, whom Hector recognized as a junior executive, half carried a female from the office and handed her off to another woman who escorted her to the ladies' room.

"Is he dead? Is he dead?" A man's voice demanded.

By now Hector was very curious. He walked slowly toward the chaos, trying to see over the shoulders of several employees who were filling the doorway. Sprawled back in his chair was Jonathan Sullivan, the Director of Finance. Blood trickled down the left side of his face, staining his neat white shirt collar. The hair near his temple was singed, and the skin was blackened from the muzzle blast. On the ceiling hung bits of Sullivan's skull cap. Pulpy brain matter oozed like clumps of sludge down the wall. His arm hung over the left side of his chair; a revolver lay several feet away. From where he stood, Hector surmised it was probably a .38 caliber.

"Move," a hoarse voice commanded as two police officers pushed their way through the crowd. Immediately Hector returned to his office, quickly gathered up his briefcase and headed for the stairwell. In all of the confusion, he knew no one would notice his leaving. Before getting into a silver Mercedes which had replaced his earlier Cadillac, he carefully removed his jacket and laid it on the rear seat. It would take a few minutes for the air conditioning to kick in, and he wanted to be comfortable for the drive home. He needed to think about the incident.

What had happened? Obviously Sullivan had killed himself. But why? Hector had occasionally worked with the man since being retained as a consultant; however, he knew very little about Sullivan. In fact, almost nothing. He did know that the man was married for he had commented on photos Sullivan kept on his desk. A wife and three kids. Problems at home? That could be the case. Hector knew from his own experience and conflict with his father when he was young that all families had problems. Maybe Sullivan was ill, but he always appeared to be in good health and, as far as Hector could remember, had never complained of illness.

He shook his head in disbelief. What a rotten thing to have happen. Suicide, and from all appearances it had to be suicide, always brought on a lot of questions. Obviously, there would have to be an inquest, but it shouldn't involve him. He wasn't a regular employee—merely a consultant.

It was still early when Hector arrived home. He changed into swimming trunks and, after a brief swim, lounged beside the pool. He had been invited to a dinner party in West Palm Beach by an acquaintance in the company, but he had a few hours to relax. Perhaps someone at the party would have additional information about Sullivan. If not, he would have to do a little investigating himself. Still, he would not rest easy until he learned more about the incident.

The Thursday after Sullivan's suicide, Hector returned to the utility company. He had a couple of hours free between consultations and planned to finish installing the software he had begun on Tuesday. It seemed to him that all of the employees were unusually subdued.

"Vicki, how's the morning shaping up for you?" Hector inquired of the receptionist at the reception desk. He always stopped and chatted with her for a few minutes whenever he came to the company. She had started working there the same time he did, so as colleagues they shared a common bond. He noted that her auburn hair had been cut short and was perched on top of her head in tight curls—an Afro he thought—as he had seen on TV that this was a new style even for non African-Americans.

"Oh, Hector. This hasn't been a good week. You know about Mr. Sullivan, don't you?"

"Yes, I was here, but since there was so much commotion, I decided the best thing to do was just move out of the way."

"Well, then you don't know." Vicki got a conspiratorial tone in her voice. "After they took the body out, the police found a note in his suit coat. It was hanging on the back of his chair, but of course, it was all bloody and no one here had bothered to touch it."

"A note," Hector prompted. "What did it say?"

"Something about him not meaning to do it and asking to not hold it against his family. That's not the exact words, but it's close. The police have the note." She stopped for a moment to take an incoming call and transfer it to the appropriate department.

"So that's all? No clear reason why he would do such a thing?"

"No, that's all the note said, but," and Vicki lowered her voice, "the rumor is that the company suspects he was embezzling money."

"Oh, really?" Hector was not pleased to hear this. "Are the police investigating for theft?"

"No. The F.B.I.'s here. They're in with the boss now, and I understand they are going to be interviewing anyone who worked closely with Sullivan or knew him well. I've never been interviewed about a crime before."

"Well, I guess they've got their work cut out for them," Hector responded. "I'm going to be in the computer center for just a minute. I've got another appointment so I'll be back again tomorrow."

Hector walked down the hall, ducked into the computer room and waited for approximately ten minutes. As he was leaving, Martin Wallace, the company president was just opening his office door.

"Oh, Pentojas. I imagine you know of Mr. Sullivan's death. Special Agent Bensenberg is here from the F.B.I. doing some investigating. He may need to talk with you." Wallace indicated a man standing to his right.

Hector nodded at the introduction. "Really. I thought I heard that Mr. Sullivan committed suicide?"

"He did," Wallace replied as he and Bensenberg moved toward Sullivan's old office. "We need to make certain why."

Hector continued on toward the elevator. The F.B.I. That was not a good sign. He shook his head, trying to clear his thoughts. Vicki had said Sullivan was suspected of embezzling. That meant a thorough investigation of all financial matters. Wouldn't it be ironic if they used Cybertech's Corporate Finance 2000. "I tell you, my helping invent that program will be my nemesis," he muttered to himself as he headed into the parking lot.

By the time Hector drove to his office, his anxiety level had risen substantially. His secretary was eagerly waiting for him.

"The police have been trying to get hold of you, Mr. Pentojas."

"The police?" Hector hoped he looked suitably surprised.

"Yes. They want to question you about a suicide at the utility company. You didn't tell me there had been a suicide."

"Well, I guess I just hadn't had time, Sharon. The Director of Finance was the victim."

"What do you want me to tell the police? They were hoping to interview you this afternoon."

Hector thought for a minute. "No, I have two appointments in Hialeah. I just can't postpone them. And tomorrow I've got to be in Key Largo." He took out his pocket notebook and rifled through the pages. "Looks like Monday would be the soonest, but Tuesday would be even better, if they can wait that long. Give them a call and see what's okay."

A few minutes later Sharon came into Hector's office. "A Sergeant Brown said Tuesday afternoon around 3:00 P.M. would be fine with him, if that meets your schedule."

"Fine," Hector replied. "Call back and confirm it."

Closing the door to his office, Hector walked slowly to his desk and sat down heavily in the chair. Questions tumbled through his mind. What was happening? The police asking to interview him; the F.B.I. called in to investigate possible theft. What had made the utility company suspect Sullivan was stealing? Why would they need to talk with him? He was merely a consultant. True, he did have contact with Sullivan as that was part of his consultant's job—to set up programs for the Director of Finance. How thorough would the investigation from the F.B.I. be? If they ran a check on everything financial, they were bound to find and wonder about the nineteen cents tacked on to each customer's bill.

What should he do? That was the big question bothering Hector. Should he sit tight, assume the investigation would not be too in depth? Should he bail out of Miami as he had done at Cybertech—leave everything behind, simply vanish? He glanced around his comfortable office and sighed. His life in Miami had been very much to his liking. Still, he felt he couldn't afford to take the chance that his actions would stay hidden.

"God damn, Sullivan," he said vehemently. "Why did he have to go and commit suicide now?"

Well, what was done was done. He sighed deeply. He would have to run, and the sooner the better. "Think," he said as he rubbed his left temple. Money was not the problem nor aliases. He had gotten together a good supply of birth certificates, social security numbers and credit cards while in California as Todd Walker. He had passports in each name for travel to several overseas areas—Europe, Africa and the South Pacific. Where to go next was the challenge. Well, he could decide that issue later. Right now, he needed to get moving.

Opening his briefcase, Hector began to carefully sort through his desk and place various papers in it. There was not much. Practically anything that would be of help to the authorities about his activities or his identity was kept securely locked up at the house. The F.B.I. or the police could search all they wanted through his office files. This was a legitimate business, a good business actually, and he suddenly felt a sense of pride. He could succeed legally; however, and he smiled briefly, he could get rich illegally.

"Mrs. Gleason," Hector said as he emerged from his office shortly before noon. "Remember I have to go to Hialeah today, and I'd better get going. I may be back in the late afternoon, but in case I get tied up, don't worry. I'll go on to Key Largo tomorrow and then see you next Monday." As he went out the door, he called back, "Any problems, tell whoever it is to hold off until next week. Have a nice weekend."

As he drove toward his house, Hector carefully outlined his next moves. First, he would immediately erase all lines of communication between his overseas accounts and the money coming in from the utility company. He would need to destroy any link in his home office to what he had been doing as he suspected the authorities would eventually be swarming through his house. A week, he thought, even if they are really good, it will take them at least a week to stumble onto what I've been doing at the utility company. But he didn't delude himself. He would be found out. It was just a matter of time now.

He would cancel his appointments in Hialeah and Key Largo himself. In this way, no one would call Mrs. Gleason to check on his whereabouts, and it would give him two days to get things in order in Miami. He needed to draw money out of his business checking accounts and close both them and a small savings account at a local bank. This would tide him over for several months until he could get relocated.

Arriving home, Hector immediately got busy with his plans. Shutting down his home computer, he took the hard drive and immersed it in the pool. Later he would toss it into one of the many canals which dotted the

Miami area. Any records, and he kept very few on his illegal business, he burned in the den's massive fireplace, along with the few computer diskettes which sizzled slightly as they melted.

The sun was setting, casting a hazy vermillion glow over the patio, as he finally began to nibble on a sandwich of cold cuts. He gulped some iced tea and realized for the first time that he was sweating. Calm down, he thought. Everything is under control. Control! He laughed aloud. He thought everything was under control for good. He was in control; it was the other people who were not. He could count on himself. Once again, he couldn't anticipate other people's behavior. How could he have predicted that after he was able to get into the utility company, some jerk like Sullivan would decide to do himself in. "Shit, shit, shit," he said angrily.

Hector continued to sit for several hours on the dark patio, mulling over all possibilities. Finally, he got up and strolled back into his house. He had liked this house; he had wanted to stay here in it. It had suited his present lifestyle and one he had hoped to continue. Now, he noted that he was thinking of his home and Miami in the past tense. His days in Miami were ended; he needed to get on with his life.

The next two days were busy ones for Hector. He took care of the required money matters; then he selected a few items of clothing and packed a bag. He looked sadly at the paintings he would leave behind. Perhaps some day he could replace them. Calling the number for American Airlines, he inquired about flights.

"Yes, sir," the pleasant voice of the reservations clerk

responded to his inquiry. "We can get you in first class on flight 327 to Boston on Saturday morning. What name will the reservation be under?"

"Sullivan," Hector replied. "Jonathan Sullivan!

"You're in row 3 in first class, Mr. Sullivan." The flight attendant indicated as she took his boarding pass.

For a moment Hector was startled. He had almost forgotten that he had taken the name of the dead Director of Finance. By now he no longer resembled a Cuban in his mid fifties. The gray in his hair had been replaced with a dark brown dye and the limp was gone. Dressed in a well-cut light gray suit with a beige trench coat tossed over his arm, he appeared to be a thirty-five-year-old executive.

After a breakfast of eggs benedict and several cups of coffee, he had time to completely read the Miami Herald before the plane reached its destination. As the plane taxied to the terminal he noted that it was spitting snow.

God, he hated snow. He had always hated snow. However, he had chosen Boston as an intermediate location for two reasons. First, it would give him time to decide on his next destination, and secondly, he needed to lose his Miami tan and permanently modify his appearance. Winter in Boston would be the perfect place to do that because he would not be going outside much.

Retrieving his one piece of carry-on luggage, Sullivan took the elevator to the bar in the airport tower. Sipping a Rusty Nail, he stared out across the bay. Gray clouds blending in with the horizon presented a bleak picture, cold and forbidding. Maybe Europe, he thought. Maybe that was it. Go over the ocean.

"You wouldn't have a phone book handy?" he asked the bartender.

"No, sir. But there's one next to the pay phone, just over there."

Sullivan looked up the number and dialed the Copley Plaza Hotel. "I'm looking for a room for the next two nights. I thought I'd be taking a plane out today, but this meeting is going to have to continue all weekend," Sullivan explained to the desk clerk. "Do you have anything available for tonight and Sunday?"

Fortunately the Copley Plaza could accommodate Sullivan. After renting a car, Jonathan fought his way through traffic to the hotel and registered. His light-weight suit and poplin trench coat was no match for the Boston weather. Immediately after checking in, he walked to Filene's and purchased a heavy coat, several sweaters and some wool slacks. He also visited a good men's store and selected several suits which meant he would have to return as they needed alterations.

By now it was late evening and Jonathan was hungry. The desk clerk recommended the Bello Mondo which was nearby in the Prudential Center. Sunday Jonathan spent most of the day in his room planning. He would need a place to stay, but for how long? Probably a month, at least enough time to lose his tan. Already several store clerks had commented on it. He had told them that he was just out on business from L.A. Early Monday morning he called a travel agency and inquired about lodgings on the coast.

"Well, Mr. Sullivan, many of the motels are closed for the season." The woman at Snoopy's Travel Agency sounded like she thought Jonathan should know this. "However, I'm sure I can find you something. How long did you intend to stay?"

"At least a month, maybe a couple of weeks longer," Jonathan replied.

"Oh, a month. Are you here on business for that long?"

"Of a sort. I'm a writer, and I need a quiet place to do some work."

"I'll do some checking and get back to you."

Within the hour the agent had done so, indicating that she had "just the thing" for him. "It's a house south near a place called Fourth Cliff. It's completely furnished, right on the ocean, and most of the other places will be closed up. So you should have your privacy."

Jonathan arranged to make payment and pick up the key to the house. He stopped on his way down Route 128 and did some grocery shopping as the agent had mentioned that many of the restaurants in the area would also be closed. It was dusk when he arrived at the beach house, which, as the agent had said was right on the ocean. The furnishings were average—early American sofa and chair together with miscellaneous attic pieces. He wondered what Georgette De Angelo would make of this place.

Quickly he got the heat up and fixed himself a salmon

steak for dinner. There was a television set, but somehow he wasn't in the mood for entertainment. He still had not decided what his next move would be. California was out. Arizona would be warm, but there was little in the way of opportunities to add to his bank roll. However, he wondered, did he need to add money? He had checked his accounts before leaving Miami and found to his satisfaction that they totaled over twenty million. "Shouldn't be greedy," he said to himself. Besides he knew now that he could make considerable money legitimately.

The main problem was the F.B.I. He knew they wouldn't give up looking for him easily once they found his trail. He doubted that they would make the connection with the name Jonathan Sullivan, but just in case they did, he should leave the country. Where to go? Tomorrow he would see if there were a library in the area and read up on several places in Europe. Italy. It would be warm in Italy or maybe Spain or Greece. It was usually moderate along the Mediterranean.

"**C**huck, how the hell are you?"

Dylan knew it was Bart Bensenberg. Only Bensenberg had ever called him Chuck. He was surprised to hear from the F.B.I. agent. It had been over six months since he had called him for help.

"I'm fine, Bart. What's new with you?"

"Well, I've got something I think will interest you."

"You've found Proteus," Dylan asked immediately.

"Can't say for sure, but it looks like we might have. We were called in on an embezzlement case for the utility company in Miami. Not for this Proteus, if that's what you mean. The Director of Finance had killed himself, and the company thought he was stealing."

"Was he?" Dylan inquired.

"No, as a matter of fact, he wasn't. He was just having an affair with one of the office employees. But, as we attempted to interview some of the employees and support staff, a consultant came up missing. His secretary didn't know where he'd gone. His home was abandoned, and all of his other appointments had been cancelled or he hadn't kept them. No one knew where he had gone or what had happened to him."

"Everything still in the house," Dylan asked. "Looked like the man just vanished from the face of the earth?"

"Exactly," Bensenberg retorted. "We had one of our computer experts examine his programs at the utility company and guess what? This guy, Hector Pentojas, had programmed the billing cycle to charge an extra nineteen cents on every customer's bill in the greater Miami area. It's got to be the scam of the year! Maybe of the century."

"Jesus, Bart. That's almost exactly what Bill Robinson did at Cybertech, and you say his name is Hector Pentojas now?"

"Yes, as a matter of fact I even briefly met the man about a month ago."

"A young man with blonde or light brown hair?" Dylan asked.

"No, a middle-aged Cuban type with graying hair and a limp."

Dylan thought for a moment. Could it be Proteus? "I don't suppose you have any idea where he could be now, do you?"

"Nope. But we did find his car at the airport, and we're checking the manifests now."

"A blue Caddy? " Dylan asked. "He had bought a Cadillac."

"No, a Mercedes. Guess he was coming up in the world, what with his added income." Bensenberg chuckled.

"Did anyone at the airport remember someone who resembled...

"Pentojas," Bensenberg interrupted.

"Yeah, Pentojas. Did anyone remember seeing him?"

"No, Cubans are a dime a dozen down here. Why would he stand out in the crowd?"

"O.K. I'm not sure he would have gone out as a Cuban anyway. He flew in and out of L.A. in a disguise and then became a blonde beach bum," Dylan added. "I'm going to fly out to Miami. I'll be there tomorrow morning."

"I'll have someone meet your plane if you call and give me the flight. Maybe between us we can find something to go on."

As Dylan and Bensenberg pulled up to Hector's home, Dylan noted the neatly trimmed yards, the homes placed well back from the street, the palms lining the street, their fronds swaying in a gentle breeze.

"Nice area," Dylan remarked.

"One of the best," Bensenberg answered. "This guy was no piker."

Hector's lawn was shaggy and the house itself had a slightly musty odor. Obviously, it had not received any attention since Pentojas had cleared out. Bensenberg followed Dylan as he wandered from room to room. Not too shabby Dylan thought. He admired the decor, the muted earth tones. In the master bedroom closet, he pawed through the clothing still hanging neatly. "Must be a fortune in suits here," Dylan commented. "It doesn't appear that Pentojas thought he would be leaving any time soon."

"No," Bensenberg agreed. "Something spooked him, and it must have been the knowledge that we would uncover his scheme when we investigated Sullivan."

"Look at the art work." Dylan pointed to a beautifully framed painting hanging over the bed. "That isn't a Holiday Inn special. That, and the others I've seen here, cost a bundle."

"And he just left them," Bensenberg shook his head.

"Well, if what you say is true, he had to move in a hurry. However, I remember that his wife told me he was very interested in art."

"Do you think he'll send for some of this stuff, or come back to pick it up?"

"No!" Dylan replied emphatically. "If this guy is my Proteus, he's not sentimental. He left his mother, his wife, a beach house with similar trappings. When he feels it's time to go, he goes."

"Well, I don't think there's much else here for you to see," Bensenberg began.

"Wait a minute," Dylan interrupted. "What about a computer. There might be some information on it. Did he have a computer?"

"Oh, yeah. There was one. Or at least there was a computer desk, and we found what looked like the remains of melted diskettes in one of the fireplaces. Haven't located the hard drive though."

"Well, he could have tossed that anywhere—a dumpster, the ocean, anywhere. He'd be smart enough to get rid of it."

"Pentojas had a computer at his downtown office," Bensenberg offered. "We checked it, but it was routine stuff. Strictly legitimate business as far as we could tell."

"No one else he was stealing from?"

"Not that we know of, but, of course, we may never

find out unless someone or some company comes forth with information about a loss."

"What about his secretary," Dylan inquired.

"A part-time person. Worked only four days a week short hours. She said he was a great boss, easy to work for, not in the office a lot. She was shocked to find out she was no longer employed. As far as we can tell, she knows absolutely nothing."

"That checks out," Dylan remarked. "He's never used an accomplice before. Doesn't need one. He's a loner—a clever loner."

The two men walked back through the silent rooms. Before leaving Dylan punched the redial button on the living room phone. The number rang numerous times before a recorded message stated: "Please stay on the line. An American Airlines representative will be with you shortly."

"Good thing you're checking the airline manifests, because apparently that's the way Pentojas left," Dylan said.

"But as whom?" Bensenberg asked. "You told me he alters identities as frequently as a chameleon."

"True, but the last two times he flew in and out of L.A., he used the alias of Mark Proteus. See if that name appears again on any of the manifests leaving Miami. For anywhere, I guess. Probably some place warm. Both his wife and another woman mentioned to me that he said he liked a warm climate."

As Jonathan Sullivan, Proteus spent several snowy afternoons in the local library. He read extensively on all of the countries in Europe with warm climates. He even did some research on Algeria and Morocco but decided quickly that they were not for him. Actually, he leaned toward Spain or Southern France. The big drawback was the language. He could muster a little Spanish, but it would take quite a bit of study to become fluent, and he wished to stay for a time wherever he decided on.

I wonder, he thought, as he looked out his window at the swirling Massachusetts snow. I have always gone to a warm place. Maybe that's too predictable. Maybe a cooler climate. However, after researching Sweden and Norway, he knew they were not for him.

"England it is," he said aloud. He could speak the language; the culture was similar to that in America; there were large cities where he could lose himself if he so chose. "England, it is," he said again.

Making a trip into Boston, Proteus purchased several pieces of good leather luggage. This time he would not need to leave his clothing behind. At a phone booth in the foyer of a nearby restaurant, he dialed American Airlines and set up his reservation. "First class, four weeks from now, if possible," Proteus said politely. "And the name is James Smythe. Smythe with an 'e'."

Bensenberg had gone back to the regional office, leaving Dylan to try and locate a trail. Dylan had been thorough. He had himself talked with Sharon Gleason. That got him nowhere. With Bart's help, he had been given access to employees and records at the utilities company. Nothing!

In desperation Dylan decided to look at the airline manifests again. Both Bensenberg and he had checked them closely for a Mark Proteus, a Todd Walker, a Bill Robinson. He couldn't imagine that Proteus would use his real name—Joshua Petersen—and he hadn't.

One more time, he thought, as he began going down the seemingly endless lists of names. By now he had determined that his target always flew on American Airlines. At least that had been the one constant so far. About six pages into American's manifests, he found it— Jonathan Sullivan. No! Dylan thought. He wouldn't have done that. But why not? It was as good a name as any, and certainly neither he nor Bensenberg had thought to check out the name of Sullivan.

Sullivan had flown to Boston. That didn't fit. Joshua liked warm climates, and the current temperature in Boston was zero. Of course, he didn't have to stay in Boston. He could merely have flown in there and then on to Houston or even back to L.A. "He'd have the guts to do that," Dylan said aloud. "And I'd never find him in L.A. if he did that a second time."

Briefly, Dylan thought of going to Boston but changed his mind. Hell, Sullivan could be anybody now, could have gone any place. He was stumped. Before going back to L.A. he decided to call Bensenberg and at least report on his Boston find.

"Sullivan?" Bart exclaimed. "You don't say. Clever of him to use the dead man's name. How'd you find it? I thought we had done a comprehensive job on those manifests."

"Just lucky," Dylan explained. "Caught my eye."

"God, that guy is cunning." Bensenberg emphasized the word "cunning."

"Yeah, tell me about it. I thought of going to Boston but decided against it. For one thing, I have to get back to classes. I can't spend all of my life trailing a specter."

"Well, let's do some thinking here," Bart began. "Why would he go to Boston? You said he liked warm weather."

"I know, and he does. I think he's changing his modus operandi, probably to throw anyone off the trail. Just in case anyone is still looking. I imagine he did this for your benefit. He knows the F.B.I. is involved in the Florida case."

"So where's he going from Boston, Chuck?"

Dylan winced at the name Chuck. "Can't say. He could go back to L.A. He's done it once, and we didn't find him."

"Yeah, but I don't think that's what he's going to do, Maybe..." Bart let the sentence hang in mid air.

"How about Europe?" Dylan interjected.

"Good thought. But where in Europe? Europe's a big place. Are you fancying a holiday in Europe? Besides, what languages does he know?"

"Can't say. I don't think anyone ever asked that question. I assume he only speaks English. I hope he only speaks English."

"Well, that may narrow the chase—England, or he could just move over the border into Canada."

"Jesus, I've been looking for him now for more than four years, and I still know almost nothing about him. How can a guy cover his tracks so easily?"

"Nothing much to it," Bart replied, "as you have found out. If I were he, I'd go to England, but since most European countries have almost everything in English to accommodate tourists, he could live fairly comfortably anywhere."

"Thanks a lot, Bart," Dylan said wearily, "That really boosts my morale. But, I do appreciate you calling me about the Miami problem and spending so much time with me. I hate to give this up, but I guess I'm going to call it a day. I've reached an impasse on Proteus and his agenda."

"Keep in touch," Bart ended the conversation. "I'll do the same if anything else turns up. But I wouldn't hold my breath."

Wearily Dylan boarded his plane for L.A. Barbara would be happy to have him stay at home for a change, and he was looking forward to getting back to the classroom routine.

THE SCOTTISH DECISION

(JANUARY 1986)

Five weeks later, flying as passenger James Smythe, Proteus peered out the window as the plane glided toward Heathrow. He could see the Thames, grey and bleak. Nearby the Tower of London and Big Ben came into his view. It appeared that the rooftops stretched to the skyline. An impressive city, he thought, but dingy, with the accumulated grime of centuries. Over the hum of the engines a child could be heard whining back in coach. Glad I don't have to put up with that, Proteus thought.

Immediately after recovering his luggage, he exchanged several hundred dollars of U.S. currency for pounds. He knew he would need considerably more, but he didn't want to draw attention to himself by asking to have thousands exchanged. He would arrange transfer of funds later to a bank. He also had false credit cards to fall back on in an emergency, but he did not want to use these.

Descending into the bowels of the underground railroad, Proteus located the train that would take him to Green Park Station. *Mind the Gap.* "These English have a strange way of telling you not to fall in a hole," Proteus muttered to himself as he stepped on to the train.

English efficiency got him to his destination in no time. "If everything could be as predictable as the British railway, I would have no problems," he thought, shaking his head slightly. With a little pushing and shoving Proteus arrived at street level. Piccadilly was always busy with activity. Head east to Piccadilly Circus, head west three blocks to the hotel. He had the directions down pat.

Shortly before leaving Boston he had reserved a room at the Green Park Hotel on Half Moon Street, just a park away from the palace. He could have stayed at the Ritz, which was a block away from the station, but it was too popular, too many celebrities, too many photographers. He acquired some rail passes to help ease his travel around the country. Some time would be needed for him to make a decision about whether he would remain in London or move on to a smaller shire. For the next few days, he became a tourist—relaxing as he took in some of the sights in both England and Wales and striking up a conversation with other sightseers to see where they had been and which location they liked best.

Sheffield didn't appeal to him. It was too industrial, although it was near Sherwood Forest. Chester was more to his liking, a friendly town near the Welsh border. "It's loaded with history," he thought, as he wandered through the narrow streets and crossed bridges which had been built by the Romans. Somehow none of the places seemed just right.

One night while he was dining at the Bryn Cregin in Wales, he struck up a conversation with the proprietor, Eric Mason, who happened to be originally from Los

Angeles. The man had flown in bombers as a ball turret gunner during World War II, had married a Welsh national and ended up buying a hotel. "Edinburgh is where you want to go next," Mason said. "Lots of sights, beautiful city, close to the Firth of Forth." The clinking of glasses and china could be heard in the background.

"Can you recommend a hotel for me?"

"More wine sir?" The waiter interrupted. "How 'bout some dessert sir?"

"No thanks." Proteus said as he turned back toward Mason.

"Sure, the Bruntsfeld. It's not too expensive, and it seems to cater to mature couples rather than large, noisy families."

He had thanked Mason for his advice and headed off to bed. The next morning he caught the early train to London, had a leisurely breakfast on the train complete with linen and silver, and returned to his room at the Green Park. "It's time," he thought. "I need to settle somewhere, at least for a while. I'll give Scotland a look."

Checking the mirror of the mahogany wardrobe in his room, he was pleased with the reflection. Blue eyes peered out from a pale face acquired from his five weeks of hibernation at Massachusetts's Fourth Cliff. His salt and pepper hair was now back to its normal brown, thanks to a color rinse. It would still be several months before all of the fake grey was gone. He sighed. It was good to be his old self, the way he had looked when Bill Robinson disappeared from Houston four, nearly five years before. Always having to be in a disguise could be tiring.

Late in the afternoon of the next day, he checked

out of the hotel and caught the night coach to Scotland. He should be in Edinburgh early the following morning. Following Mason's advice, he had booked a room at the Bruntsfeld.

Stepping into the lobby of the very old building, it was obvious that technology was not the priority. The carpet was a dark red and the walls were an even darker tone. The pub was just off to the left of the lobby and was decorated with the proverbial bagpipes and putters. Scotland, the birthplace of golf. "I'll have to visit St. Andrews" Proteus muttered to himself.

"Welcome to Edinburgh, Mr. Grant," the young female desk clerk chirped after noting his signature on the guest register. "Connor Grant. That's a good Scottish name. Are you from the Grant clan?"

"I think so. That's why I'm here. Tracing back the old family tree." Proteus liked his new name. It had a solid sound.

"Good luck," the woman replied as she handed him a key and indicated where his room was located.

Since he had not slept well on the train, he took a short nap, arising in time for a late dinner at Deacon Brodies, a dark smoky pub with the traditional local cuisine. The next day he roamed through some of the remaining stone paved streets of Edinburgh, visiting the palace of Holyrood house and admiring the old paintings of various Scottish royalty. During succeeding days, he visited the house of John Knox, St. Giles Cathedral and ended one day at Edinburgh Castle. Again, he found the town citizens friendly and helpful. There was a relaxed feeling to Edinburgh. He could see why Mason had recommended the city. Still, he felt he wanted to see more of Scotland before he made a final decision whether to stay there or return to London.

After a week, Connor took a trip up to Inverness. Since it was about eight hours by train or automobile from Edinburgh, he had to stay overnight. Again, he was impressed by the town; however, he felt it was too small so that his presence might draw undue attention if he were to settle there. In addition, it was very remote and did not provide an easy escape route in case he needed such.

"Okay," he thought. "What are the 'pluses' for Edinburgh?" He could speak the language fairly well; the city was large enough so that he could become relatively lost; there were many exit routes. The large airport would facilitate his going to London and onto the continent where much of his money was hidden. Glasgow, a large city, was also close at hand. The climate would be the only real drawback. Still, he had lived in warm places for many years. If anyone were ever to look for him, they would probably not zero in on Scotland. "Maybe I'll get me a tartan," he said aloud. "Just become one with the natives."

Quickly he began to make plans in his mind. Scotland would be perfect. He now had a new place, a new name and it was the beginning of the New Year.

For several more weeks Connor wandered around Edinburgh, learning the street names and checking out various housing areas. Every day he visited a different pub, casually chatting with the customers over a pint of ale. One day, quite by accident, he strolled into the King James Inn, a small out-of-the-way establishment on Candlemaker Row.

'Not quite up to the king's standards." he thought as he settled at the bar. The dark paneling went well with the dark Guiness. Huge beams, which reminded him of railroad ties spanned the ceiling. Several faded tartans, a golf bag and a bagpipe adorned the walls. "Seedy" was the adjective that popped into Connor's mind.

"Not too many customers today," he said pleasantly to the man behind the bar.

"No. It's off season."

"Oh, I hadn't thought of that," Connor responded.

"You a Yank?"

"Yeah!" Connor took a swig of the Guiness.

"Just over for a holiday?"

"Haven't made up my mind," Connor glanced around the pub. "I may decide to stay for a while."

"Well, it's a great place," the man added.

"Yes, I concur. In fact, I've been giving some thought to going into the consulting business."

"Consulting? What's that? What do you consult about?"

"Oh, computer consulting. That type of thing," Connor explained.

"Well, I could sure use a consultant—not a computer man, of course—but someone to help me get this place turning a profit again."

"Problems," Connor asked, more to pass the time rather than probing for knowledge.

"Yes, I'm the proprietor of this inn. Angus Fitzroy's the name." He extended his hand after wiping it off on a bar towel.

"Connor Grant," Connor said, shaking Fitzroy's hand.

"Grant? From the clan?"

Connor didn't know what he should say. Finally, he smiled. "Could be."

"Well, welcome home," Fitzroy beamed as he moved off down the bar to welcome another patron.

Home. That was a thought that hadn't entered Connor's mind. Why not? This guy was obviously in need of financial help. The place could use some money to bring it back to life, and he had money—plenty of it. He had pretty much decided to stay in Edinburgh. It would be home, unless some stinking human went and screwed his agenda up again. But, he needed some type of cover. He was still a fairly young man. Even though he would not be too flashy with his spending, people would wonder how he was wealthy enough to be idle. He needed to work. Why not switch from computer consulting to landlord? It might be interesting to help run an inn. He would stay in the background, let Fitzroy still be the front man and no one would think that odd. He would merely have invested in a legitimate business. He looked around the room again. He was smart. With a little work, he knew he could make Fitzroy's King James Inn turn a tidy little profit.

Over the next several weeks Connor slowly cultivated his relationship with Fitzroy. A giant of a man, Angus was big enough to wrestle an ox. He was the epitome of a Highlander with wiry red hair that draped over his broad shoulders and a booming laugh. Eventually, Connor mentioned that he was considering investing some money in a business in Scotland. Fitzroy took the bait and casually mentioned that he might like to have a partner. He would continue the day-to-day management of the Inn, and Connor, if that was his desire, could remain conveniently in the shadows.

The venture into the King James Inn had been a successful one. Connor and Angus were compatible partners, and the inn's clientele had grown steadily over the years. Angus had been only too happy to have most of the financial problems of an aging hotel lifted from his shoulders. During the first year of the partnership Connor had funded a complete renovation of the three floors of guest rooms, the lobby, restaurant and pub. The utilities had been brought into the twentieth century while the decor was still rustic Scotland. Then Connor had set about getting the inn listed in the tour brochures as a three-star establishment—not the top of the line but certainly very acceptable to the average traveler. Angus was impressed by Connor's insight into what it would take to make the inn profitable, and he watched each year as the number of guests rose steadily upward.

Meanwhile Connor had gradually assimilated into the Edinburgh culture. He had purchased a cottage off Dean Street and hired an elderly widow to clean and to prepare some of his meals. Over a period of time Fitzroy had introduced him to some of the other businessmen, and, as the inn prospered he became a respected member of the business community.

However, Connor did little of the day-to-day management of the inn. He had not accumulated millions to work eight hours a day. After the third year his share of the profits were more than adequate to fund a fairly luxurious lifestyle for Edinburgh. Unfortunately, he still could not afford to be conspicuous with the millions he had in reserve, so he had to use his fortune cautiously. Because he wished to splurge—after all, why have money if you can't spend it—frequently he traveled on holidays to the Continent, especially to Paris and Geneva. Frequently he spent a weekend in London. Occasionally he indulged his passion for art and purchased a few good pieces from "up and coming" young European artists. These he displayed in his home for his pleasure and, from time to time, for a few select guests. In this way he could enjoy his stolen funds without everyone questioning his source of income.

Again, his biggest problem was not being married. As with his past identities he found himself the victim of matchmakers. However, he was again able to solve this problem. During the time he was transferring money for the purchase of his home, he had been helped by one Catherine Macleod. A thirty-one-year-old University of Edinburgh graduate, Catherine had foregone marriage to pursue a career in finance. Short and trim with hazel eyes and shoulder length brown hair which she wore swept back in a French twist, Catherine also had expedited numerous transactions for the inn. As a "thank you" for her help, Connor had invited her to lunch on several occasions. Over the course of a year they had developed a comfortable relationship. They often went boating on the Firth of Forth with several other couples.

Her parents had invited him to dinner a few times, and he was impressed by their home which, he was told, had been in the family for seven generations. Although it was modest by American standards, the ancient stonework and the leaded windows gave him a sense of how solid Catherine's childhood had been, totally unlike his own. Both Mr. and Mrs. MacLeod seemed to like him and also seemed glad that their daughter had, as Mrs. Macleod put it, "a gentleman friend."

Although Connor had absolutely no interest in religion, now and then he would accompany Catherine to services at St. Giles cathedral. He disliked sitting through the lengthy service and chatting with everyone afterward; however, the church attendance provided an acceptable routine for his new identity and, as an added asset, helped business.

Catherine was interested in art and music, so often on weekends they would take the train to London to see a musical or visit a museum. At first, since this usually necessitated staying in London overnight, they had reserved separate rooms. Still, both were mature adults, and it was not long before they were registering as a couple. Spending late evenings with his arms wrapped around Catherine, Connor enjoyed his natural male drive, and the two spent the nights making love. Connor had been fairly abstinent since he left Margaret, except for a very brief encounter in California with Rhonda just before her untimely death. However, he had always been very careful not to do his thinking from between his legs.

As time progressed, Connor knew that friends and acquaintances assumed that eventually the two would marry. He admired and liked Catherine. She was smart and clever. Like Connor she was interested in having enough money to live comfortably. This, she once explained, was the reason she had not married. She had seen many of her friends marrying young and living poor.

As time passed Connor could see hints that Catherine was considering marriage—to him. This presented a very real dilemma. He was now content with his way of life. There had been no hint of anyone from the United States questioning his past, so he had begun to feel safe from being discovered. On the other hand, he wasn't sure he wished to be all alone forever. Yet he was loath to trust anyone. If he married Catherine, would he be able to trust her completely if she knew of his past? If not, would he be able to keep his true identity hidden? She obviously was aware that he had an adequate income; how could he explain the large amounts of additional income which his millions provided in interest alone? Actually, because he didn't wish to appear pretentious or have his income appear suspicious, he didn't even take all of the interest his nearly twenty-seven million generated. Could he keep these financial assets hidden from her? He recalled only too clearly finding Tina Zabinski rifling through his mail. Of course, Fitzroy had been quick to tell anyone who asked that his partner was a rich American who had made millions in the computer business. No one had ever questioned his source of money—at least not to his face.

Finally, Connor reached a decision. "Catherine," he began as they dawdled over dessert one late summer evening in 1992, "we've been 'courting' as some of the old folks say for several years now. I guess we should make the arrangement permanent."

"Oh, Connor. Aren't you the romantic one? Was that a proposal or were you suggesting some business merger?"

"You can't be surprised, Catherine," Connor replied. "I guess it isn't the movie type proposal, but we get along well together, and," he added as he gazed out at the darkening sky, "neither of us is getting any younger."

"So, am I marrying a rich man?" Catherine asked, with a gleam in her eye.

Connor realized that Catherine probably had heard rumors of his wealth or wondered for years why he was able to transfer large sums of money from various banks. Still, she had never questioned him on this until now. But why should she need to; she had access to his bank account and she knew the money was there. How or when it was gained should be of no concern. Also Catherine had seen his home, and as far as he knew had never been "blabby" about his finances or way of life.

"Yes, you are!" Connor answered with the slightest smirk. He was on the verge of being boastful but caught himself in time. Then he continued, "We have similar interests; we both are independent; a marriage might suit us both."

Catherine had paused for a moment, a quizzical expression on her face as if waiting for an additional comment. When none was forthcoming, she reached across the table, took his hand in hers and agreed. A few days later Connor presented her with a discreet but excellent quality diamond. Friends immediately wanted to know when the wedding would be, but both Catherine and Connor agreed upon the following summer. For Connor life was moving along smoothly.

Spring 1993

"Excuse me," the elderly man spoke softly to the desk clerk.

"Yes, sir. May I help you?" The young woman smiled pleasantly as she brushed a stray lock of auburn hair into place behind one ear.

"That gentleman that was just speaking with you, is his name Robinson?"

"No, sir. That's Mr. Grant."

"Grant?" The old man looked puzzled. "Is he an American?"

"I'm not certain, sir," the desk clerk replied. "I'm fairly new here. I believe I heard that he was from America originally, but he's been here for quite some time. He is half owner of this inn."

"Grant, you say. My wife could have sworn he was a man I worked with several years ago in the U.S. Name was Robinson, Bill Robinson."

"Really, sir," the clerk responded politely.

"Well, my wife's probably mistaken," the man said, shaking his head. "People sometimes remind you of other people. But I had to ask as my wife wouldn't let the matter rest."

The desk clerk smiled briefly, patiently waiting for the gentleman to conclude the conversation.

"Oh, well, I need you to make out my bill. Dawson's the name, Jim Dawson."

"**M**r. Grant."

"Yes." Connor turned and walked toward the check-out desk. "What can I do for you, Megan?" Megan Strother was only nineteen, had been working at the King James for a scant four months but did an excellent job of handling with courtesy and tact the harried and sometimes inconsiderate tourists. She had coal black eyes that always seemed to hide a hint of a smile and a soft voice that brought out the best in people.

"The strangest thing happened this morning," Megan began. "One of the tourists thought he recognized you as someone else – or at least his wife did."

"Someone else." Connor was instantly alert, although he lounged on the check-out desk and idly rifled through the guest register, apparently completely at ease.

"Yes. He thought your name was Robinson. Bill Robinson I believe he finally said."

"Really," Connor gave a short laugh. "Where did he supposedly know me—or this Bill Robinson—from?"

"I didn't ask," Megan replied. "When I told him you

had lived here a long time, he seemed to lose interest."

"Is he still here at the inn?" Connor asked. "Perhaps I could have a chat with him. It might prove interesting."

"No, Mr. Dawson checked out right after our conversation. He was part of the Americans Abroad group."

Dawson! The name was a blow from the past. Connor said a few more words to Megan Strother and walked out the inn's front door. Jim Dawson. Margaret's uncle! It had to be. Margaret. He hadn't thought of his wife in over a decade. By now he was certain she had either had him declared dead or filed for a divorce. What would that make Margaret, he mused, a widow? A divorcee?

Of all the bad luck, to have Jim Dawson as one of the Americans Abroad tour party. What was that old saying, "If you didn't have bad luck, you wouldn't have any luck at all." He felt as if he were in that category.

How had Dawson recognized him? True, he no longer dyed nor bleached his hair, but its normal light brown shade was naturally showing some touches of gray. He had grown a small neat moustache and now occasionally wore glasses, all of which should have helped change his identity. His voice, Megan had said. Dawson had mentioned his voice. It was difficult he knew to disguise the voice, and the way a person walked was hard to alter. He cursed himself now for having given up the limp of Hector Pentojas. The limp and use of a cane had given him an altogether different gait.

Of course, if anyone were going to recognize him, it would have to be Dawson. When he was married to Margaret, both Dawson and his wife has seen them often. Actually, very often, as they dined together several times a month. And during his years at Cybertech he had worked closely with Dawson. Damn! What should he do?

"Don't overreact; stay calm and think," he muttered to himself as he casually leaned on a stone balustrade. Connor watched as one of the employees sprayed down the sidewalk with a garden hose and straightened the tables and chairs outside the pub. The afternoon drove of patrons would soon arrive for their daily pick-me-up of ale. Across the street a small fountain sprayed mist over scarlet and gold primroses.

"Probably nothing will come of this," Connor thought. However, a familiar paranoia returned. Should he take an extended vacation into the highlands? No! He had better stay close in case someone came sniffing around. Also, he had better be prepared to abandon his lifestyle in Scotland at a moment's notice. Definitely, he would have to pay more attention to the guest register.

"**M**argaret, dear. How good to see you again." Jim Dawson kissed his niece on the cheek and ushered her into the living room.

"How long have you and Aunt Gladys been back from England, Uncle Jim?" Margaret Robinson asked as she greeted her aunt.

"About a week now," Dawson replied. "We just finally got unpacked."

"And just finally got all of our clothes cleaned and washed," her aunt added with a laugh.

The three sat companionably over a light dinner of baked halibut and cucumber aspic. After the dishes had been tossed in the dishwasher, the three settled in the den.

"I know you probably don't want to see these slides," Gladys Dawson began, "but Jim insisted that we show them to somebody. And you are the unlucky relative. It may take hours."

"I'd love to look at them," Margaret emphasized the word love. "I plan to sleep late tomorrow instead of going to church, and I would just like a lazy evening."

For the next hour and a half Jim Dawson narrated his slide presentation, moving to the screen occasionally to emphasize a point. Finally, a slide popped up of the King James Inn. Seated and standing on a terrace were a number of guests, including some of the Americans Abroad Tour. Dawson pointed out Stella Zytle who had become a close friend on the trip.

"Oh, Margaret," he suddenly exclaimed. "See that man in the background, the one to the left with the moustache?"

"Yes," Margaret replied. Very faintly she could make out the image Dawson was pointing to.

"Glady's swears that's Bill," Dawson declared.

For a moment Margaret didn't understand her uncle. "Bill? My Bill?" She finally stammered, her eyes wide in astonishment.

"Yep! I'm sure of it."

"Oh, now, Jim," Gladys immediately put in, "I thought it was when I first saw him, but I'm not sure anymore. In fact didn't you tell me the girl at the desk said that was a Mr. Grant, who owns that hotel?"

"No, you were right. It's Bill," Dawson stated. "I'd stake my life on it."

"Uncle Jim, Aunt Gladys," Margaret began. "What are you two saying? No one has seen Bill since he disappeared twelve years ago. No one could even get a trace of him. Remember, the company looked for him for years."

"I know. I know."

"But it sure sounded just like Bill," Gladys Dawson interjected. "I overheard him speaking to another guest."

"After all these years, to find Bill... " Margaret began.

"Jim," Gladys interjected. "Let's stop it. We're getting Margaret all upset, and for what? We just think it's Bill Robinson."

"Is he married, Uncle Jim?" Margaret asked in a tiny voice.

"I don't know, Margie. I didn't ask. I should have asked some additional questions. When the clerk said he wasn't Bill Robinson, I just accepted that we'd made a mistake. But the more I got to thinking about it, the more sure I became. It's Bill. He's living in Scotland."

For a few minutes all three sat silently staring at the screen, as particles of dust drifted through the beam of light and the cooling fan whirred. Finally Margaret got up and moved closer to the images. "I can't see that man clearly enough to really say, Uncle Jim. He's about the right height, I think."

"Well, I'm certain enough that tomorrow I'm going to call Mike Nolan at Cybertech."

"But they won't care now, will they?" Margaret asked. "After all, it's been so long. Besides they wouldn't hire him back now, would they? Would they bring him back here?"

"No, as you say, I doubt that Nolan will care one way or the other; however, he might be interested in just knowing that Robinson is alive. At any rate, I'm going to give him a call."

"If he is Bill, Uncle Jim, do you think he'd come back home?"

"Oh, honey," Gladys interrupted, drawing Margaret down at her side, "don't even think about that. Bill left you flat, didn't even leave a note. You don't want him back."

"I suppose you're right, Aunt Gladys." Sinking back into the couch, Margaret sighed. "Still, I'd like to know if it really is my Bill."

Around eleven o'clock the next morning Dawson finally made phone contact with Mike Nolan at Cybertech.

"Jim. Good to hear your voice," Nolan greeted the older man.

"How are things at Cybertech?" Dawson responded.

"Fine. Just fine. How's retirement treating you?"

"Well, that's why I'm calling." Dawson replied. "Retirement's fine, and my wife and I—you remember Gladys—just returned from four weeks in Europe. You'll never guess who I ran into?"

"No, who?" Nolan continued shuffling through a pile of papers on his desk. He was too busy to play guessing games with one of the firm's retirees.

"Bill Robinson!"

"What?!" Nolan dropped the papers he had been holding.

"I thought you'd be surprised."

"My God. Surprised is not the word. Flabbergasted is more like it. What did he say?" It had taken Nolan a minute to think back on the man who had so successfully stolen from the company – his company now that Vickers was also retired.

"Well, I didn't talk to him. I merely saw him. He owns a fairly prosperous hotel in Edinburgh."

"No kidding. Bill Robinson." Nolan repeated the name again.

"Did he see you?"

"I don't think so. He's going by the name Grant. Apparently has lived there for several years."

"How did you recognize him?"

"Well, Gladys heard this voice first, and I also knew I had heard it before many times. I had seen the man on the terrace when I was snapping some pictures, and I thought he looked awfully familiar then but didn't think much about it. But when I heard the voice I knew for sure."

"So you have a picture?"

"Yes, not a terribly clear one of him, but even Margaret thought it resembled Bill."

"You told Margaret that you had seen her missing husband?"

"Well, she was over for dinner and the slide show, and it just sort of came up naturally."

"O.K.," Nolan began. "Let me get my thoughts together on this. I doubt if we try to do anything. What could we do?"

"Well, I'm not totally dumb. I know you wouldn't have hired that investigator all those years ago just to get Margaret's husband back. I figured Robinson must have stolen something from the company. What was it, some fancy program?"

"You always were pretty sharp, Jim," Nolan replied. Only he, his predecessor Vickers now on the Board of Directors, and Dylan knew of the missing millions. He didn't want Jim Dawson to know of that problem. "But I doubt that we could prosecute now—statute of limitations and all that. Besides we have newer programs now. Still, if we do find out anything else, I'll be sure and call you."

"Thanks, Mike. I just wanted you to know."

"Oh, by the way," Nolan interjected before Dawson could hang up. "Could you send me a copy of the photo? I'd like to see for myself who you think is Bill Robinson."

few days after Dawson's photo arrived, Nolan drove to Pepperdine University for an 11:30 A.M. appointment with Charles Dylan.

"Been a long time since I've walked across a college campus," Nolan began as he shook Dylan's hand and followed him into his office.

"I don't have a secretary to bring you coffee like at Cybertech," Dylan began. "And I don't want to hear about how small and cluttered my office is."

It was small, Nolan noted, comparing it with his own office and the luxury it presented. Was this the usual office of a professor at a major university? He felt a smug satisfaction at having chosen a business career and all of the "perks" that went with it.

The two men exchanged a few pleasantries and commented on how each had aged a little but still looked "pretty fit" before Dylan suddenly said, "You mentioned something about me working that old case on Bill Robinson or Proteus as we finally began calling him. Are we both crazy?"

Nolan laughed. "I know it's a long shot, but take a look at this photo. Jim Dawson took it, probably by accident, when he and his wife were on vacation in Scotland."

Dylan examined the photo. "I guess it could be Bill Robinson. But it's pretty grainy. Are you sure you want me to tackle this again? It was expensive for Cybertech years ago, and it will be again."

"That's not an issue," Nolan replied. "What's it going to cost—plane ticket to Scotland and a few days per diem? Then we'd know for sure, wouldn't we?"

"Yeah, and I'd like to know. This case has bothered me for over a decade. I guess I could swing a trip away from the classroom next week, but. . ."

"Problems?" Nolan asked.

"What good would it do if I locate him? The theft is now way in the past as far as the law is concerned. He can't be arrested and prosecuted for what he took from Cybertech.

"True," Nolan replied, "although I'll bet we're not the only place he embezzled. I'll bet he's done this again and again and may be still doing it. Could be some other organization is also looking for him. If we find him, we can make inquiries through the police agencies to see if he's on anyone else's list."

Dylan didn't look convinced. "Well, you said Dawson inquired about Robinson to one of the desk clerks. Don't you think Robinson—or Grant as Dawson said he's now calling himself—is probably aware someone has recognized him? He's probably changed his identity again and is on the run."

"Could be. Maybe the trip will be wasted. But, like you,

this unfinished business has nagged me for years. And it's especially nagged Vickers. I'd like to put it to rest one way or the other. I'd like to find out if this is your Mr. Proteus and at least let him know we found him. So let's try it."

"All right," Dylan replied, "but if you want to throw away any more of your money, why don't you just go to Las Vegas?"

The following week Dylan arrived in Edinburgh and, after taking a quick shower at his hotel, found his way to the King James Inn. For two days he loitered in the area, dining in the inn's restaurant, chatting over drinks in the bar with inn guests and local patrons, and reading countless newspapers and magazines in the lobby. No one resembled the man from the wedding photo Dylan had of Cybertech's Bill Robinson nor did he see anyone who fit the description Dawson had provided. Finally, he knew his continued presence in and about the premises was becoming suspicious as it was obvious that he was not staying at the King James. He was left with a direct approach.

"I'd like to speak to the manager of the hotel, please," Dylan asked Megan Strother who was again manning the reception desk.

"Is there some complaint, sir?"

"No, I'm not a guest at this hotel," Dylan replied. "I merely would like to talk with the manager."

After excusing herself Megan went to a phone at the

rear of the desk and spoke into it for a few minutes. Shortly thereafter a portly sandy-haired man appeared at Dylan's elbow.

"You wanted to see me, sir?" Angus Fitzroy asked.

Taken aback, Dylan stared for a minute into the friendly blue eyes hidden somewhat beneath bushy brows. "I wished to meet the manager of the establishment."

"I am the manager, sir. Angus Fitzroy. Wha' can I do for you?"

"There must be some mistake," Dylan began, still confused. "I thought the manager here was a Mr. Connor Grant."

"Oh, he's part owner of the inn; however, he doesn't come around on a daily basis. I'm certain I can help you."

"Do you know where I can locate Mr. Grant? It's personal business — quite urgent actually."

Angus turned to Megan. "Please ring up Mr. Grant for me, Megan."

Dylan and Fitzroy chatted about the Scottish weather as they waited for Megan to get Connor Grant on the telephone. He could tell that Fitzroy was curious about his "personal business" with Grant, but the man was too polite to ask any questions.

"No answer, Mr. Fitzroy," Megan reported.

"Did Mr. Grant say he'd be in today, Megan."

"Not to me, sir. But often he comes by around mid-afternoon."

"Well," Angus began as he turned back to Dylan. "I don't know exactly wha' to tell you. Since we believe he will be here later in the day, you might come back around four o'clock."

Dylan could see that he had no choice but to return in hopes of seeing if Grant were really Proteus. As he hesitated, Angus asked, "Have you been to Edinburgh before?"

"No, this is my first trip," Dylan replied.

"Well," continued Angus, "in the meantime you might spend a few hours at some of our historical sites. Most people find them interesting. The Edinburgh Castle is just a short walk from here and is a most enjoyable place."

"Good idea," Dylan said, thinking that he had to pass the time some way until later in the day. "I'll get a bite of lunch and then take in the castle." He thanked both Angus and Megan and walked swiftly out of the lobby.

Going to the desk Angus spoke softly to Megan. "What was the gentleman's name?"

"I don't know, sir. He never told me his name. He just asked for the manager."

"Well, keep trying to get Mr. Grant on the telephone and tell him this American said his business is urgent. If we can't reach him, the Yank will simply have to wait until we can," Angus said as he walked away.

Almost immediately after Dylan had left the inn, Connor Grant walked in. For the past week he had been on the continent for both business and a brief holiday. Then, today, he had been to the bank transferring funds and confirming a dinner engagement with Catherine MacLeod.

"Mr. Grant," Megan Strother called across the lobby. "May I see you for a moment, please?"

"Sure, Megan. What's up?"

"There was an American gentleman here to see you. He said it was some kind of personal business—very urgent.

I tried telephoning your home but received no answer."

Connor was instantly attentive.

"An American man? Did he leave a business card?"

"No, and neither I nor Mr. Fitzroy got his name."

"Well, I can't think of anyone with whom I'd have urgent personal business. What did the man look like? Old? Young?"

"About your age. A fairly tall man. Serious. And he has very short hair."

"Is he coming back? Am I to call him?"

"He said he'd return near four o'clock."

Just then Angus rounded the corner of the lobby desk. "Oh, there you are, Connor. Megan's told you there's an American asking after you?"

"Yes, she did. Said he'd be back later."

"Well, I sent him off to see the castle. He was going to get some lunch before that."

"O.K. I'll be back later. I have a couple of errands still to take care of."

Leaving the inn, Connor immediately walked to the castle and located a spot where he could view the incoming tourists with little chance that he would be observed. Over an hour passed before he spotted a slightly familiar figure strolling toward the portcullis. For a few minutes he couldn't place the man's identity. Then it came to him. *That investigator I saw in Los Angeles. What was his name? I remember now, Dylan. He was the professor at that California university. So old Dawson had spread the word.*

"Well, damn, here we go again," Connor muttered angrily. However, he knew that getting angry would not make the man go away and would only cloud his thinking. "I guess it's time to pack up and leave town."

Connor made his way home to tidy up a few ends before leaving. He wanted to be on his way within the hour. Two small bags had been packed and stowed in a closet a month earlier, right after he had found out Jim Dawson was making inquiries. His funds always were easily accessible. With just a little urging and comments about a family emergency, he located Dylan's flight itinerary from the airlines. The investigator had purchased a round trip ticket and was scheduled to depart Heathrow in three days. Fine, he thought, that gives me time to book an earlier flight and return to the States ahead of him.

Connor got up and poured himself a bourbon and soda from the liquor cart sitting by a large leather sofa. He took a swig and looked around the comfortably furnished room. The afternoon sun filtered in through tall windows and cast a faint shadow on the thick wool rug, its muted colors providing a feeling of warmth. On the mantle over the stone fireplace was a water color of the Scottish highlands. A photo of a smiling Catherine stood at one end. Connor sighed deeply. He hated to part from this home as he had hated to part with his Florida house. His years here had been among the best of his life.

Why was this guy Dylan still looking for him after all of this time? It had been more than a decade. Could Dylan do anything at this late date except make his life miserable by blowing his cover of Connor Grant? Of course, that's exactly what was happening. No longer could Connor Grant exist. Still, he would have to make sure that Dylan was finally done searching for him. He would have to make sure that there were no more leads Dylan could use. He was tired of being chased.

He dialed the inn and reached Megan Strother. "Has the American come back yet?"

"No he hasn't, Mr. Connor."

"Well, when he does, tell him I'll meet him as close to four o'clock as possible."

"I don't know the gentleman's name, sir."

"Well, I believe it's an old friend of mine, a Mr. Charles Dylan."

"Mr. Dylan. Very good sir. I'll be sure he is informed."

Connor continued his preparations for leaving. Taking Catherine's picture from the mantle, he slowly rubbed his fingers over the glass as if to touch her face. Then he dropped the photo in one bag and loaded both bags into the boot of his auto. He didn't want Catherine MacLeod to get mixed up in his problems or have to answer questions about him. Grabbing a sheet of stationery, he paused in thought for a moment before jotting a few lines:

Catherine:

Something from my financial past has caught up with me. Enclosed is a power of attorney made out to you. Do what you will with this house and my share of the inn. It's all yours. I'm sorry to do this to you, truly sorry. I can't explain now, but perhaps one day in the distant future I will be able to make it all clear.

Forgive me,
Connor

A power of attorney was a poor substitute for a future husband, he knew, but it was the best he could do under the circumstances. It was certainly better than what he had done for his wife Margaret. He wished he could take Catherine with him, but it was impossible. It would take too long to explain the situation, and time was short. Then there was always the possibility, a good possibility, that she would not be willing to accept him when she learned the truth. Not only that, but she would slow him down. Connor sealed the note and dropped it in the post on his way to the airport. By seven o'clock he had left his car in the long-term parking, had flown under another alias to London and was settled in his room at the Green Park Hotel on Half Moon street in Westminster. In three days he would pick up Dylan's trail.

Dylan returned to the King James Inn at promptly four. Yes, Mr. Grant had come in; yes, he had been told that an American gentleman needed to see him. He had indicated that he would return for the meeting around four o'clock.

Patiently Dylan waited until six-thirty. Then he asked the evening desk clerk to see if he could locate Connor. No luck. There was no answer at his residence. No one had seen him at the inn since around noon. All Dylan could do was go back to his hotel and wait.

Early the next morning Dylan again showed up at the inn. Fitzroy and Megan Strother did their best to locate Connor. No one had seen him since the previous day. All calls to his home went unanswered. Fitzroy checked with Catherine McLeod who indicated that Connor had failed to show up for their dinner engagement. Finally Angus offered to deliver Dylan to Connor's house.

"Let us drive out to his place, Mr. Dylan. Connor has a lovely spot and a big garden. He may be out tending it and didn't hear the telephone."

It was unlikely that Grant was still in the area, Dylan knew. Grant was Proteus; he was certain. He felt a brief sense of elation. But he was gone—again! He felt certain that they wouldn't find him or anything else worthwhile at his house.

And Dylan was correct. Fitzroy finally procured a key and the two men went inside the home. Just as Proteus had done in Santa Monica and Miami, if there had been a computer, it was missing; clothes still hung in the closets; quality artwork was on the walls; the place was deserted. Dylan noted the feeling of recent vacancy.

"Damn, missed him again," Dylan said aloud.

"I beg your pardon."

"Nothing, Mr. Fitzroy. Just talking to myself."

Angus dropped Dylan off at his hotel, and Dylan explained that he could wait no longer. He would see Connor on his next trip to Europe. The urgent business would simply have to wait.

It took Dylan only a few minutes to complete his packing and be on his way to the airport. With luck he could be in London and in bed by ten o'clock. He would do a little shopping the next day before his plane left Heathrow—get a little something English for Barbara.

Connor arrived at Heathrow, caught a British Airways flight into J.F.K. and made connections to Los Angeles. Based on Dylan's flight schedule, Connor had known that he would arrive in California about fifty minutes before Dylan. He hated to admit it, but he had to admire the man's tenacity. Years had passed and the guy was still in pursuit. Somehow he had to make the man aware that he should give up the chase, that he would always be one step ahead of Dylan, always elusive.

It felt good to be back on American soil. There was nothing wrong with Scotland, of course, but over the years the many days of cloudy, damp weather could be depressing and made him yearn for his brief months on the beach in Santa Monica. Now that he was back home, he'd simply change to a new identity. He always planned for just such a necessity and had several possibilities ready and waiting. After that, he'd go into hiding for a period of time, let any trail go cold. "Then, who knows? Maybe I'll get back into the computer programming business." He smiled at the thought.

Dylan felt he had never been so tired. The trip from England was exhausting and had seemed endless. J.F.K. was always crowded, and, since his overseas flight had been running a little late, he had to scurry to make his connection to L.A. He stood in the aisle of the 747, crowded by the people getting up from seats behind him and reaching for parcels in the overhead bins. Finally he was able to make his way into the main terminal and head for the baggage carousels.

"Mr. Dylan. Mr. Charles Dylan. Please pick up a white courtesy phone," a voice crooned.

Who could want me on the phone, Dylan thought. Barbara was not planning to meet him in L.A. as he had his car at the airport. Maybe it was Nolan. He stepped off the escalator, scanning the walls for the courtesy phone. Locating it, he leaned on the wall as he picked it up.

"This is Charles Dylan."

"Hello, Mr. Dylan. I understand you have been looking for me."

"Who is this?"

"I believe you know me as Bill Robinson, Anthony Stevens, Mark Proteus, Todd Walker, Hector Pentojas, Jonathan Sullivan and most recently Connor Grant of Edinburgh Scotland." The man's voice held a hint of laughter.

Dylan was stunned. "Where are you?" he finally managed to get out.

"Look over your right shoulder at the white courtesy phone near the exit."

Dylan looked across the crowd milling around waiting for their luggage and saw what appeared to be a middle-aged man in a dark blue suit. As their eyes met, Dylan knew he had finally found his man. "Proteus!" he said aloud.

"Quaint name," Proteus said as he grinned and hung up the phone.

Instantly Dylan dropped the phone, scrambled through the recently arrived passengers, hurriedly grabbing their luggage. "Excuse me. Pardon me. Please, let me through," he repeatedly exclaimed as he pushed and shoved his way toward the exit. "Please, get out of my way!"

By the time he reached the door, Proteus had disappeared in the direction of the cab stands. Dylan rushed outside, only to catch a glimpse of a blue suit disappearing into one of many Yellow cabs. He had never before felt so helpless. Standing in the dusk he watched the red glow of the cab's tail lights as it pulled into the line of Los Angeles traffic. From out of the back window an arm waved in a final salute.

Printed in the United States
75726LV00001B/37

9 781583 851159